The

FIRST STATE OF BEING

ERIN ENTRADA KELLY

The
FIRST
STATE
OF BEING

 Greenwillow Books
An Imprint of HarperCollinsPublishers

The author would like to thank Hamline MFAC faculty, especially Laura Ruby and Elana K. Arnold. Thanks to Colby and Adie Robinson, Lindsay Burgess, Teresa Bonaddio, Sara Crowe, Hugo Heriz-Smith, and sneaker connoisseur Terry Horstman. Eternal appreciation to the team at Greenwillow, especially (and always) Virginia Duncan.

To Sharon Huss Roat and Danny Eaker: enough love and gratitude to cross every timeline.

The First State of Being

www.harpercollinschildrens.com

The text of this book is set in Iowan Old Style.
Book design by Sylvie Le Floc'h

Library of Congress Cataloging-in-Publication Data
Names: Kelly, Erin Entrada, author.
Title: The first state of being / by Erin Entrada Kelly.
Description: First edition. | New York : Greenwillow Books, an Imprint of HarperCollins Publishers, 2024. | Audience: Ages 8-12. | Summary: When Ridge, a time-traveling teenager from the future, gets trapped in 1999, he befriends Michael, a lonely twelve-year-old boy, changing the course of their lives forever.
Identifiers: LCCN 2023053851 (print) | LCCN 2023053852 (ebook) | ISBN 9780063337312 (hardcover) | ISBN 9780063337336 (ebook)
Subjects: CYAC: Time travel—Fiction. | Friendship—Fiction. | Single-parent families—Fiction. | Filipino Americans—Fiction.
Classification: LCC PZ7.1.K45 Fi 2024 (print) | LCC PZ7.1.K45 (ebook) | DDC [Fic]—dc23
LC record available at https://lccn.loc.gov/2023053851
LC ebook record available at https://lccn.loc.gov/2023053852
24 25 26 27 28 LBC 5 4 3 2 1
First Edition

 Greenwillow Books

***

To the Laughing Man

***

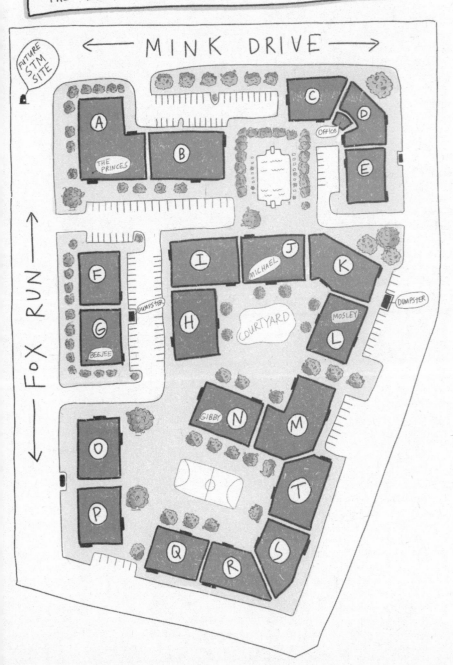

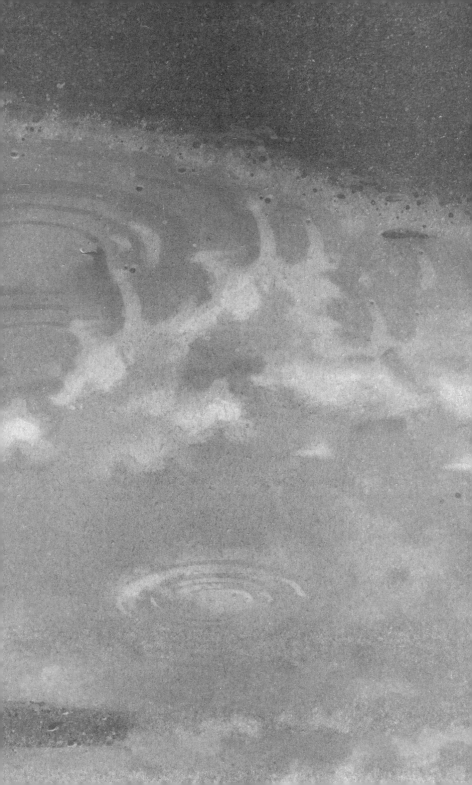

The
FIRST
STATE
of BEING

Y2K, aka the Millennium Bug or the Year 2000 Problem, refers to a worldwide panic that occurred on-world as the calendar neared January 1, 2000. At the time, it was believed that computer systems would malfunction when internal program systems reset to the year 00. Some information technology experts warned that computers would not be able to distinguish the correct meaning of 00, resulting in widespread failure of vital infrastructures. This failure was expected to cause disruptions in air travel, banking, industry, electric grids, phone systems, and other critical services necessary for daily living at the turn of the century.

The Y2K scare was fueled by intense media coverage. Ultimately, however, there were very few disruptions, and no disaster came to pass.

Excerpt from The Spatial Teleportation Summary Book for the Turn of the Twenty-First Century (1980–2020), *compiled by Maria Sabio, PhD, DST, Chief STS, University of Delaware, translated from Original Eaker Linton Code*

1

*P*eaches, Michael Rosario thought. *That's what we need.*

His mother loved peaches.

If the world came to a standstill at midnight on January 1, 2000, at least she would have two things she cherished: peaches and Michael.

He gazed at the shelves of canned fruit in Super Saver. He pulled the can from the shelf. He looked left. Then right. Then left again. It was early—barely seven thirty in the morning—so the place was practically empty. It was the perfect time to go grocery shopping.

If you'd call it that.

He slipped the peaches into the pocket of his windbreaker and felt them settle. He focused on the exit and headed in that direction. He pictured his mother, huddled in the darkened hours of the new millennium, scooping a spoonful of sweet peaches into her mouth, saying, "You know what, Michael? You were right about Y2K. I should have listened. Sometimes eleven-year-old boys know exactly what to do."

Only he wasn't eleven anymore. As of today, he was twelve. And they probably wouldn't need to open the canned goods right away. They'd have to eat everything from the refrigerator first before it all went bad.

The exit was right in front of him—one or two steps and *shoop*, the automatic doors would slide open—

"Hey-hey, Mikey-Mike."

He froze.

It's Michael, not Mikey-Mike, he instinctively said, though he didn't say it aloud, because he recognized the voice and it belonged to nineteen-year-old Billy Gibson, who everyone called Beejee. If Michael were a different person, he might have kept walking or pretended he hadn't heard, but he couldn't—of course he couldn't—because everyone always heard Beejee. Beejee made sure of that.

Michael turned.

The peaches were so, so heavy.

Michael felt the urge to sneeze—he was still getting over his stupid summer cold—and his eyes watered. He didn't want to move, he didn't want to sneeze, he didn't want to do anything but disappear into the ether.

Beejee was in the produce section wearing the standard Super Saver uniform, the same kind Michael's mother had worn before she'd been fired. A cart of potatoes was parked next to him.

"What're you doing here so early in the morning?" Beejee said. He picked up some potatoes and shoved them into place. "Getting flowers for your mama?" He snickered.

Michael couldn't think of anything to say. Not a single word came to him. He pressed his right thumb into the center of his left palm. *As soon as he looks at the potatoes again, I'll keep walking,* he told himself. But Beejee didn't look at the potatoes. Instead, his gaze drifted over Michael's shoulder and landed on Jamar Prince, who was walking toward them holding three Butterfingers and a crumpled receipt.

Beejee's expression turned serious.

Jamar smiled faintly at Michael. "Hey, I thought that was you," he said. "You wanna walk back with me?"

Since when did Jamar Prince, who was sixteen and in high school, want to walk anywhere with him? Since when did Billy Gibson work the morning shift? Since when did either of them come anywhere near the Super Saver at seven thirty a.m.? Michael was here at precisely this time because he didn't want to see anyone, and now look.

"Um." Michael shifted from foot to foot.

Beejee strode over holding a pale white potato, which somewhat resembled the shape and color of his head. He narrowed his eyes at Jamar's candy bars. "Did you pay for those?"

Jamar raised his chin. "Yeah, I paid for them," he said, his voice sharp. "What're you trying to say?"

Michael's body tensed. He felt like a blade of grass caught between two boulders.

The exit was right there. A few steps away.

"If you paid for them, how come they're not in a bag?" said Beejee.

"What do I need a bag for?" Jamar said. "And I don't need to steal candy bars from this raggedy store when I have money of my own." Jamar stepped closer to Michael and nudged his shoulder. "Come on, let's walk back. Keep me company."

Jamar headed toward the exit.

Michael followed.

"You better not be stealing! My father's the manager, you know!" Beejee called after them. He was talking to Jamar, of course, even though Michael was the one with a pocket full of peaches.

Jamar called Beejee a name under his breath—a two-syllable swear word—as he and Michael went through the automatic doors and walked toward Fox Run Apartments, where they both lived.

Michael wasn't one for swearing. He heard it all the time, of course—at school, around the complex, in movies—but for whatever reason, it made him feel squirmy. Like he was doing something wrong, even though he wasn't doing anything.

"I wanted to make sure he wasn't giving you a hard time," Jamar said. He shoved two of the candy bars in his back pocket, ripped the third open with his teeth, and spit a piece of the torn wrapper onto the ground as they crossed the street. Michael wanted desperately to pick it up so he could throw it away properly, but he didn't want to look fussy. Jamar continued. "Sometimes he messes with Darius."

Darius was Jamar's youngest brother. Michael wasn't sure how old he was. Maybe eight or nine. Jamar had another brother, Elijah, who was going into seventh grade, just like Michael. They weren't friends. They weren't enemies. They weren't anything.

"Darius is quiet, like you," Jamar said, his mouth full. "Easy target for people." Except he didn't say "people." He said the swear word again.

They were now on the grounds of Fox Run Apartments and Townhomes—The Best Community in Delaware!—and Jamar veered left, toward Building A, while Michael veered right, toward Building J.

"See you around," said Jamar.

"Thanks," Michael said. But Jamar was already too far away to hear him.

Michael didn't realize how tense he was until he saw the courtyard near his building. He took a deep breath and relaxed his shoulders. Everything looked as it should. Cars in their assigned parking spots; a stray cat, the one Michael had secretly named Tuxedo, slinking around the bushes; Mr. Mosley, the maintenance man, hefting a can of paint toward a vacant apartment.

"Hey, Mr. Mosley," Michael said.

Mosley looked up. He had a brown, weathered face, smattered with wrinkles and folds from his forehead to his chin, but when he smiled—like he was doing now—all the lines settled at the corners of his eyes. He was wearing his painting coveralls with *Fox Run* stitched on the pocket.

"Michael!" Mosley said cheerfully. He set down the can of paint. "Just the man I wanted to see." He pulled out his wallet, the one with the Philadelphia Eagles logo emblazoned on the front, and slipped a crisp twenty-dollar bill from it. "Today is your big day, if I'm not mistaken." He waved the money in Michael's direction.

"You don't have to give me anything," Michael said. He sneezed and wiped his nose with the back of his hand—

something he'd never do if his mama were here. But Mr. Mosley didn't care about such things.

"Well, yeah, I don't *have* to. There are only two things I *have* to do: pay taxes and die," Mosley said. One of his favorite expressions. "Actually, make that three things: pay taxes, die, and paint 3F." He toed the paint can. Eggshell white, it said. Same color in every apartment. "But for right now, I'm giving you twenty bucks."

Michael wanted to take it. But he also *didn't* want to take it. It's one thing to shoplift because you don't have money. It's another thing to shoplift when you do.

That's how Michael reconciled it, anyway.

Maybe I'll walk back to the Super Saver later and pay for the peaches properly, he thought, even though he knew he wouldn't.

"Thanks, Mr. Mosley," Michael said. He took the money.

"No problem. Besides—"

Mosley stopped mid-sentence.

There was a kid, a teenager, several paces away, wandering toward them with an unusual expression on his face. He kept glancing over his shoulder, like he was being followed. He looked . . . what? Not afraid or panicked, exactly. More like someone who had just committed a crime. Robbed a bank, perhaps, or stolen canned goods from Super Saver. As he came closer, Michael realized how odd his clothes were. He was wearing a uniform of some kind. Shirt and pants. White, but not white. Eggshell, maybe. Like the paint. And his shoes were exactly the same eggshell color. Together, the outfit glinted strangely in the sun.

Mosley stepped in front of Michael.

"Hey there," Mosley said. "Can I help you?"

The teenager seemed startled that Mosley was speaking to him, even though Mosley and Michael had been watching him the whole time and vice versa.

"Hello," the teenager said. He looked like he could be half Filipino, like Michael. He stopped on the sidewalk a few steps in front of them and cleared his throat. "What's up?"

"You need help with something?" Mosley said.

"No. I mean, yes?" He paused. "My name is Ridge. It's a pleasure to meet you."

Mosley ignored the introduction. "You need help with something?"

"Could you tell me the date?" Ridge said.

"It's August seventeenth," Michael said quietly.

"Thank you," Ridge said. He glanced over his shoulder. "Of what year?"

Michael glanced at Mosley. What kind of person didn't know what *year* it was?

"It's 1999," Mosley replied, more a question than a statement.

Ridge repeated the year under his breath. The expression

on his face changed. Excitement or fear; Michael couldn't tell which.

"You live here, at Fox Run?" Mosley said. "Never seen you around before."

Ridge didn't answer. He was chewing his bottom lip like he was trying to solve a complex math equation.

"Did you hear me, kid?" Mosley asked.

"Yes. I mean, yeah," Ridge replied, walking backward, like he couldn't wait to get away from them. "I do. I live right around here." He waved in a general direction that didn't mean anything. Then he turned on his heel. "Thanks for your help! Peace out!"

Mosley and Michael watched him disappear behind Building F.

"Well, that was weird," Mosley said. He picked up the paint can. "Better keep an eye on that kid if we see him around again. He's up to something." He punched Michael playfully on the shoulder. "Then again, we're all up to something in our way. Right, Michael?"

"Yeah," Michael said, thinking about his pocket of peaches. "We're all up to something."

2

It was nearly eight a.m. when Michael sailed through the front door to find his sixteen-year-old babysitter perched on his secondhand couch. Gibby. Arms crossed, eyebrows raised, brown eyes blinking at him. A paperback of *Last Act* by Christopher Pike sat facedown on her lap, its spine creased. The smell of strawberries permeated the air. He wasn't sure if it was shampoo, body spray, lotion, or what. Michael blushed.

Did all sixteen-year-old girls smell like strawberries, or just Gibby?

Just Gibby, probably.

As far as Michael was concerned, Gibby was the only reason Fox Run Apartments were the "best community in Delaware." She lived in Building N.

"You have some explaining to do, mister," Gibby said. "Today is a babysitting day. I got here at 7:30 sharp, and you weren't here. Your mother specifically said—"

"My mom didn't tell me it was a babysitting day."

"—that you are not supposed to leave this apartment when you're home alone."

His mom couldn't afford to pay Gibby every day. Instead, she picked days here and there throughout the week. Michael made it his business to know which days were Gibby days and which weren't. He wished all of them were, even though twelve was way too old for a babysitter.

"So? Where were you?"

"Uh . . ." He shifted his eyes away from her face.

She tapped her foot. She had small, narrow feet tucked inside pink sandals.

He couldn't say he'd gone to Super Saver. If his mom found out, he'd be in trouble. But Beejee had seen him, and Beejee was Gibby's brother. (Michael still couldn't figure out how the world's most perfect creature could be related to a rotten potato like Beejee, but these were the mysteries of the universe.)

Michael decided to go with a half-truth.

"I was talking to Jamar Prince," he said. Gibby went to high school with Jamar. If she thought Michael was friends with Jamar, maybe she wouldn't see Michael as such a kid.

"About what?"

Michael paused. "Nothing, I guess."

She was still staring at him with her eyebrows raised, so he continued. "Then Mr. Mosley and I saw a weird guy outside."

"What kind of weird guy?"

"I don't know, exactly," Michael said. He wasn't sure where to begin. The strange outfit? The fact that he didn't know what year it was? The way his eyes darted around before he said "Peace out"? Michael shrugged. "Just weird."

Gibby uncrossed her arms and leaned forward. "Well, you're still not supposed to leave the apartment alone. Especially if some weird guy is wandering around. But . . ." She sighed dramatically. A mischievous smile spread across her face. "I *suppose* I'll let you off with a warning, since it's your birthday."

Michael's heart raced. "You remembered!"

She set her book aside and revealed a wrapped gift she'd hidden under the cushion. Michael leaped forward, beaming, and took it—with too much enthusiasm, probably, like a kid. But he couldn't help himself. He tore it open and let the wrapping paper fall to the carpet.

"The new Red Hot Chili Peppers CD!" Michael announced, as if she didn't know what she'd given him. "Yes! Thank you!"

Gibby stood up and hugged him. Before he could decide how to hug her back, she'd let go. The entire world was now alive with strawberries.

He swallowed.

"You're welcome," she said. "What's the point of working at Circuit City if I don't use the discount?"

Michael turned over the CD and read the list of tracks aloud, one by one.

Surely it meant something that she'd gotten him a gift, right?

And it was a Red Hot Chili Peppers CD too, which was his favorite band.

She remembered his favorite band *and* his birthday.

That had to mean something.

3

Mosley rang Michael's doorbell at noon on the dot. When Gibby opened the door, he came in with three bologna sandwiches—two for him, one for Michael—and a packet of Skittles for Gibby.

"Make sure to tell your mom we had a nutritious lunch," he said to Michael as he settled down on the one wobbly stool at the kitchen counter and popped open a can of Dr Pepper, his favorite drink.

Mosley was the first friend Michael and his mama had made when they moved to Fox Run. When Ms. Rosario was working, which was almost all the time, Mosley stopped by to make sure Michael hadn't been kidnapped by psychopaths or brainwashed by daytime television. At first, Mosley pretended like he was there to fix something, like the dishwasher or the refrigerator, but he eventually abandoned the charade, and now he just came over for lunch.

Mosley took a bite of his sandwich and turned toward Gibby, who was reading her book with the bag of Skittles next to her.

"What book you got there, kiddo?" Mosley asked, talking with his mouth full.

"It's called *Last Act*, by Christopher Pike," Gibby said. She looked up, eyes bright. "It's about this group of seniors who put on a play at school about a murder. And then, on opening night, the leading actress is *actually murdered*. This girl Melanie is accused of doing it, because she fired the gun and everything, but she didn't *actually* do it, because the gun was supposed to be a prop. Now she has to find out who the *real* killer is before her life is, like, totally ruined."

"Sounds interesting," Mosley said. He swallowed. "I can't remember the last time I read a book. I was probably Michael's age. Fifty years ago, now. Man, time goes fast."

Gibby gasped. "You haven't read a book in *fifty years*?"

"Never had reason to, I guess."

Michael stood at the counter eating his sandwich quietly, trying to imagine Mr. Mosley as a twelve-year-old.

"You can borrow this when I'm done," Gibby said, turning

the page. "It's so good! I won't say anything else about it. That way I won't spoil anything."

"A book might make good company," Mosley said.

Mosley had been married once, a long time ago, but now he lived alone. He'd never had kids.

Michael finished his sandwich and brushed the crumbs off his hands. "Did you see that weird guy again, Mr. Mosley?"

"Yeah, I saw him," Mosley said. "Something's off about that kid. Can't put my finger on it. If he lingers around too long, I'll have to tell Mr. Ship. Hate to do that, though. Just in case."

"Just in case what?" Michael asked.

"Just in case he's harmless. Don't wanna get him in trouble if he's some innocent kid going through a hard time. I remember what that's like."

"What if he's not an innocent kid, though?" Michael said. It was easy enough to imagine an endless series of dangerous scenarios. They clicked through Michael's mind like scenes in a movie. *Sociopathic teenager burns down apartment complex. Sociopathic teenager attacks innocent twelve-year-old shoplifter. Sociopathic teenager kidnaps beautiful sixteen-year-old babysitter who smells like strawberries and loves mystery novels.* Click, click, click.

"Don't worry," Mosley said. "I'm sure it's nothing." He took another bite of his sandwich. "I bet he's gone by tomorrow."

4

At three o'clock, Michael and Gibby left the apartment to feed the cats.

They weren't supposed to. Mosley had warned them dozens of times that the apartment manager, Mr. Shipman—who everyone called "Ship"—would "read them the riot act" if they ever got caught, but Michael couldn't stand the thought of the cats going hungry. "Cats never go hungry," Mosley had said. "They're survivors."

But Michael would lie awake at night, imagining each and every one of them—perhaps some he'd never even seen—wandering the world alone. In his imagination, they were always sad. Hungry. Meowing into the darkness, waiting for someone to notice them.

He couldn't sleep sometimes because of it.

So they fed the cats. It wasn't a gourmet meal or anything. Just cheap stuff in pull-tab tins from Dollar General. Better than nothing, though.

They had a routine. Michael put fresh tins under the bushes in front of Buildings N, M, and L and collected the empties in an extra plastic bag while Gibby tagged along.

They had moved on to Building L when Michael decided to tell a small lie.

"I might go out for sports this year," he said.

"Really?" Gibby said.

Michael reached behind a bush and retrieved the can they'd set out last week.

"Yep," he said, tossing the empty can into the bag. "Maybe football."

"Football?"

"Yeah," Michael said, wiping his hands on his jeans. He didn't like the look she was giving him, even though it was the same look he'd give himself if he was in her shoes. Or sandals, as the case may be. "Why? You don't think I'd be good at football?"

He pulled the lid off a can of Best Feast.

"It's not that," she said. "It just . . . doesn't seem like your thing."

A question immediately sprang to Michael's mind: *What*

do you think is my thing, then? But he didn't ask. He wasn't sure he wanted to know the answer. Instead, he set the Best Feast in its spot and said, "It could be. My dad is an athlete, you know. Or he was. Maybe he still is."

"I didn't know that."

"He played basketball for Villanova."

"Just because your dad is an athlete doesn't mean you have to be," Gibby said. She gathered her hair in a ponytail and secured it with a blue scrunchie.

"I know," Michael said.

"So why do you want to do it then?"

Michael shrugged with one shoulder. A squirrel darted into their path.

"I don't know," he said.

But he *did* know.

If he played football, people might like him. Girls, even. Girls like Gibby.

No one had ever liked him before. Not like that. Not like anything, really.

They silently changed out the cat food in front of Building L, then meandered toward the dumpster to get rid of the empty cans. Michael kicked absently at the cement as they walked, trying to think of something smart to say.

Maybe I should ask her about her book, he thought.

"Who is that?" Gibby said.

Michael looked up.

It was Ridge. He was standing very still, staring at the dumpster with his nose pressed in the crook of his arm.

"That's the weird guy me and Mr. Mosley were talking about," Michael said, slowing down.

"What's he doing?"

"I have no idea. Let's turn around," Michael said. "We'll just go to another dumpster."

"Oh, wait. He saw us," Gibby said.

She was right. Ridge was looking at them, jogging their way.

"Hello, what's up?" he said. His voice was odd. Stilted. He stopped and motioned to the garbage behind him. "Can you tell me what that is?"

Gibby raised an eyebrow. "What, the dumpster?"

"Dumpster," Ridge repeated.

"It's where people put their trash?" Michael said.

Mr. Mosley's words echoed in his head. *Something's off about that kid.*

"Oh," Ridge said. He laughed nervously. "I know. I was just joshing."

"Um. Okaaay," Gibby said.

Michael wanted to leave. He didn't want to be near someone who was *off*. The whole thing made him nervous. But instead of walking away, Gibby said, "What were you doing over there, anyway? You looked hypnotized."

Ridge glanced back to where he'd been standing, as if he'd see himself there.

"Oh, that? I was just . . . I don't know, studying it? The smell is terrible."

"That's because it's *garbage*," said Gibby.

"Word."

"Word?" Gibby asked, puzzled.

"I mean . . . yes. It's garbage." Ridge nodded toward their bags and frowned. "Is that plastic?"

"Yes," Michael said.

"Plastic *garbage*," Gibby noted. "I'm Gibby, by the way. This is Michael."

"I'm Ridge," Ridge said. He ran his fingers through his hair.

Gibby pointed at the nearest building. "Do you live there?"

"I'm new around here, you could say," Ridge said. "Which building do *you* live in?"

He stuck his hands in his pockets and smiled. It changed the tenor of his face. Suddenly he didn't look so *off* and menacing. In fact, he looked friendly, which only made Michael more nervous.

Gibby laughed. One loud "Ha!"

"Like I'm going to tell some random guy which building I live in," she said.

"You asked me first," Ridge said. Still smiling. "What about you, Mike? Which one—"

"It's Michael, not Mike," said Michael. He turned to Gibby and held up his bag of empty Best Feast cans. "I'm going to throw these away."

Michael may have only *just* turned twelve, but he knew one thing for sure: there was something strange about a guy who was hypnotized by garbage and didn't know what year it was.

Thankfully, Gibby followed him.

As with all timeprints, the late twentieth century—defined here as 1980 to 1999—developed its own slang, some of which evolved from earlier timeprints, and others that were influenced by popular culture, primarily music. Spatial Teleportation Scientists should avoid interaction with Native Timeprint Inhabitants (NTIs); however, if scientists are engaged in unavoidable conversation, they should be aware of popular slang being used at this time in order to have an organic, seemingly natural conversation.

The slang used in this timeprint could depend on the age of the NTIs, their race and/or ethnicity, and/or their geographic location; therefore, the following should be considered generalities for young NTIs in the United States during this period.

What's up? A common greeting, especially among young people. If an NTI says "What's up," do not take this literally. Instead, assume the NTI is asking how you are and/or what you are doing.

Later. A common phrase of departure among young people. Can be used interchangeably with "Goodbye." Other common phrases of departure in this demographic include "Peace" and "Peace out."

Not even. This translates to "I don't agree with you." Typically used in friendly conversation. Can be used interchangeably with "No way," in which the person would counter with "Way."

No duh. This phrase would typically be spoken when someone has said something obvious.

Let's bounce. This should not be taken literally. It means to leave or depart.

Word. Confoundingly, this typically means "I agree," but is also used to mean many other things. It can be a question, for example, such as "Word?" The scientist is advised to simply repeat "word" back to the speaker and/or to consider the context of the conversation before providing an appropriate response.

Bad/baddest/badder. When used as slang in this timeprint, bad often means good. However, good never means bad. Good means good. Bad means "exceptionally good."

Excerpt from *The Pop Culture Omnibus (1990–2020)*, by Maria Sabio, PhD, DST, Chief STS, University of Delaware

5

The world would shut down at midnight on January first. Michael knew it. Everyone knew it. People couldn't stop talking about how computers would automatically glitch when the year switched from 1999 to 2000. Electricity grids, airline flight controls, phone towers, all of it. Michael's mother didn't seem worried, but Michael knew she was too busy working three jobs to truly consider the implications of Y2K. That was why Michael was preparing for both of them.

At least once a week, he sprawled flat on the worn carpet of his bedroom to count the canned goods and other supplies he'd secretly stored under his bed. That's what he was doing now, as he listened to his Red Hot Chili Peppers CD on his portable stereo. He had it turned up even louder than usual because Gibby was in the living room and he wanted her to know how much he loved it.

There were four cans of green beans. Three cans of peas. Chef Boyardee, five cans. One package of crackers. Two bags of trail mix. And one can of peaches. He mentally counted the days until Y2K. Fourteen days left in August. Thirty days in September. Thirty-one in October. Thirty in November. Thirty-one in December. That totaled one hundred and thirty-six.

The last song ended as he got up off the floor. Good thing too, because his mother would be home soon and she was *not* a fan.

Even though Ms. Rosario worked three very different jobs, she kept the same schedule each week, which comforted Michael because he always knew where she was at any given time. From seven a.m. to noon on Monday through Friday, she worked at Little Rascals Day Care. On Wednesday through Sunday, she was a server at Chi-Chi's Mexican restaurant. On Mondays and Tuesdays, she picked up the two to nine p.m. shift at Danneman's Fabrics.

Once upon a time she had been a shift supervisor at Super Saver, and she'd only needed one job. But that was before Michael ruined everything.

Tonight, though, she wouldn't be working until nine. She'd promised she'd come home early for his birthday and they'd watch television together. And she always kept her promises.

Michael sat on his bed and fell back on his pillows as silence filled the room. There was a small water stain on the ceiling. Michael stared at it and thought about Gibby, quietly reading in the living room. *Maybe I'll read that book too,* he thought. Then they could talk about it.

The front door clicked open just after seven. Michael heard the muffled sound of his mother's voice. Thanking Gibby, no doubt, and giving her a few dollars.

"I don't need a babysitter," Michael said, to the water stain. But one second later, he hopped up, threw open the bedroom door, and called out, "Thanks for the CD!" Even though he'd already thanked her.

Gibby was almost out the door. She gave him one last "Happy birthday!" Then she stepped outside just as his mama turned toward him with a Foot Locker bag dangling from her arm.

"Birthday boy!" she sing-talked. Her name tag hung loosely on her shirt. GLORIA. "I have a special delivery for you!"

Michael smiled and joined her on the couch. "How was work?" he asked.

She smelled like the restaurant, but Michael didn't mind. If his mother was home, he was happy, even if she smelled like chimichangas.

"I took every breath," she said.

It was what she always said. *I took every breath.* In other words: if she was still here, still breathing, it was a good day, and she was thankful for it.

She placed her hand on his forehead. "Still no fever. Looks like you're all better. And I've got something that might bring you to a full recovery. Ta-da!" She presented the Foot Locker bag.

Michael beamed. "Thanks, Mom."

He pulled out the box. It'd be nice to have new sneakers, even if they were off the clearance rack. When he lifted the lid, he expected to find a half-decent, unpopular design that had been marked seventy-five percent off. He did not expect a brand-new pair of Air Jordans, size eight. But that's exactly what he saw.

"What," he said.

This was an even bigger surprise than the CD.

He stared at the shoes. "But how?"

She kissed his head. "It's your birthday," she said.

"But . . ."

Air Jordans were expensive. Really expensive, like a hundred and fifty dollars. And they didn't have a hundred and fifty dollars. Just the week before, they'd dug through the couch cushions looking for loose change for the laundry.

"You're starting a new school soon," she said. "You need

to look sharp. The only bad thing is, people will be looking at your feet instead of your beautiful, adorable face."

She squeezed his cheeks between her hands.

"But . . . ," he said again, thinking about the neat stack of monthly bills on the kitchen counter and all the Y2K supplies they could buy with a hundred and fifty dollars. "How . . ."

"It's your birthday," Ms. Rosario repeated cheerfully. "And this is your birthday gift."

Michael blinked at the shoebox. They had bills, true. They needed to be better prepared for Y2K, yes. But Michael wanted the sneakers. He'd never had Jordans before. Most of his wardrobe, with the exception of a few favorite T-shirts, was secondhand. But these brand-new Jordans smelled so . . . well, *new*. Like they'd been plucked from the Nike warehouse just for him.

Ms. Rosario wrapped her arm around his shoulders. "All you have to do is say thank you."

Michael swallowed.

"Thank you," he said.

Michael put the sneakers on right away. As soon as he heard the thrum of his mom's shower, he went to his room, turned on his portable stereo, and walked around the apartment, letting the music settle into his bones as his feet adjusted to the miracle of brand-new Air Jordans. He wanted to wear them every minute, for the rest of his life.

He wandered to his bedroom window and looked out, just because.

The courtyard between apartment buildings was deserted, except for a single person sitting on one of the benches.

Ridge.

Clipper, the stray cat with the clipped tail and patch of missing fur, was sitting on his lap. Clipper was one of the sweetest strays at the complex. She loved to get scratched behind the ears. She'd lived a tough life but still trusted people, somehow.

Michael thought of Mr. Mosley's words again—*something's off about that kid*—then snatched the cordless phone from the kitchen and called Gibby.

"Hey," Michael said as soon as she answered. "That guy Ridge is outside on the bench right now."

"So?"

"So, he has Clipper on his lap." Michael rushed back to his room to look out the window.

"He has *who* on his lap?"

"One of the cats."

"So?"

"So, Mr. Mosley said there was something off about him. What if . . ."

What if he hurls Clipper across the courtyard? What if he yanks Clipper's tail, just to hear him yowl? What if—

"I'm gonna go out there and see what he's up to," Michael said. There was a twinge of uncertainty in his voice, but he meant it. He turned off his music. "I mean, he was fascinated by *trash*. And did you see his clothes? There's something wrong with him. Something *off*."

Gibby sighed. "No. Don't. I'll go." There was rustling on the other end of the line.

"You shouldn't go by yourself," Michael said. "What if he's a killer or something, like in one of your books?"

"I'm sure he's not a killer," she said, like that was the most ridiculous thing anyone could have said. "I'll call you back."

After she hung up, Michael returned the phone to its cradle, tightened the laces on his Jordans, and knocked lightly on the bathroom door.

"I'm going outside for a second, Mom," he said. "I'll be right back."

"Okay," she said, her voice muffled. "But don't be too long. *Wheel of Fortune* starts soon."

"I'll be back by then," Michael said. Under his breath, he added, "I hope."

There have been numerous theories of time put forth by leading modern scientists, such as A. Saeed, L. Daystrom, D. Noonian, S. Huss-Roat, et. al. (see *Theories of Time*), but it is generally unknown how the disruption of time may influence past, present, or future events, or the nature of time and space itself. Spatial Teleportation Scientists (STSs) refer to this as the unknown factor. Because of the unknown factor, STSs must develop a reasonable and responsible hypothesis before engaging in spatial teleportation. However, it is likely that we will never understand how spatial teleportation influences the timeline until and unless STSs engage in active teleportation.

Should the Global Science Council choose to move forward with spatial teleportation, it is critical that STSs preserve the integrity of the existing timeline and reduce potential adverse effects of the unknown factor by adhering to best practices, which are as follows:

1. Do not reveal information about things to come, especially if NTIs have a reasonable ability to manipulate said events. In cases where NTIs do not have a reasonable ability to manipulate events, it is still best to withhold all information.

From Best Practices for Responsible Spatial Teleportation (ST)
by Maria Sabio, PhD, DST, Chief STS, University of Delaware

6

Michael's apartment was closer to the courtyard than Gibby's, so he got there first. He didn't like arriving first anywhere. It usually meant he'd have to talk one-on-one with someone he didn't know, which was pretty much his worst nightmare, whether they were a cat-murdering psychopath or not. But there was nothing he could do about it now, because Ridge looked up and saw him.

"Hello," said Ridge. "What's up?" He moved over on the bench. "Want to sit?" Clipper darted off. Michael watched him go.

"Uh." *Not at all.* "I guess."

He sat down just as Gibby came into view, wearing her favorite oversized University of Delaware T-shirt.

"Is this a meeting place?" Ridge said when he saw her. "A place where people chill?"

Something about Ridge reminded Michael of assemblies at school, when they'd invite a grown-up to talk about drugs or stranger danger or whatever, and the speaker would try to sound like one of the students. To be "cool." But Ridge wasn't a grown-up, so it didn't seem to make sense.

"How old are you?" Michael asked.

Before Ridge could answer, Gibby sat down. "Where's the cat?"

"He ran off," Michael said.

"I'm sixteen," Ridge said. He eyed Gibby's T-shirt. His face lit up. "You go to UD?"

"No," Gibby said. "I'm sixteen. I go to Red Knot. Where do *you* go?"

"What do you mean?"

"Where do you go to school?"

"My mother teaches me."

"Like, homeschooled?"

"Something like that," Ridge said.

"I'm going to UD when I graduate," said Gibby.

Michael wondered if he'd go to UD when he finished high school. He hadn't even started seventh grade yet, so college felt like a world away. Maybe Gibby would be interested in him when he got to college. Maybe they'd even be in college at the same time. *Maybe I'll study something really smart, like business or economics.*

"My mom works there," Ridge said.

"What does she do?" Gibby asked.

"She's head of the STS department," Ridge replied.

"What is STS?" Michael asked.

"Spatial—" Ridge stopped abruptly and pressed his lips together. "I don't know. Something, something."

A few silent seconds slipped by before Gibby said, "So listen—we were wondering . . . do you live in the complex, or . . ."

Ridge paused. "It's complicated."

"So you do, or what?" Gibby said.

"I live here, but I also don't live here."

"Are you homeless?" Gibby said. "Like, you live on this bench or something?"

"Homeless?" Ridge said, like he didn't know what it meant.

"Let's make this easy," Gibby said. "Where *exactly* do you live?"

"I live with my mom in faculty housing on the Red Knot campus at UD," Ridge replied matter-of-factly.

"There *is* no Red Knot campus at UD," Gibby said.

"Not yet," Ridge mumbled.

"What do you mean, not yet?" said Gibby.

Michael glanced back toward his apartment. His mother was probably on the couch, waiting for him. She'd taken off early from work and everything. Michael considered leaving, but a series of disasters click-click-clicked through his mind. Ridge kidnapping Gibby. Ridge hypnotizing Gibby and forcing her into a cult. Ridge and Gibby falling in love because no one was there to distract them.

Time to say something. Have a voice in the conversation, Michael.

"You're being very mysterious," Michael said.

"I know," said Ridge. "But I can't say anything. I mean, I shouldn't. I *want* to. But I shouldn't."

"*Why* shouldn't you?" Gibby asked.

"Are you in witness protection or something?" Michael offered.

"No," Ridge said.

"Are you a wanted fugitive?" asked Gibby.

"No."

Michael: "Are you hiding from someone?"

"No."

Gibby sighed. "*What*, then?"

"I can't say. I mean, I shouldn't." Ridge raised his eyebrows. "Could you tell me how to get to the mall?"

"The *mall*?" Gibby said.

"Yes. The mall. Don't you have buses or Ubers or something?"

"What are Ubers?" Michael asked.

"We're not telling you anything until you answer our questions," Gibby said.

"But . . ."

"But what?" Gibby said.

"But if I tell you who I am . . ." Ridge paused, measuring the rest of his sentence.

"If you tell us who you are, *what*?" Michael said.

"It might destroy the universe."

Gibby snorted. "You certainly have a high opinion of yourself."

"I'm being serious."

"So am I," Gibby said.

Ridge looked at Michael, then Gibby, then Michael, then Gibby. "If I tell you who I am and where I came from, you'll think I'm delusional."

"We already do," Gibby said.

"You have to promise not to tell anyone," Ridge continued. "Not a word. Whether you believe me or not."

Gibby raised her right hand. "Promise."

"Okay," Michael said, a few beats behind. He didn't raise his hand.

"All right. Here goes," Ridge began. He considered his next words. "I guess you could say I'm not exactly from around here."

Gibby motioned toward his eggshell-colored mono-chromatic clothes. "Duh."

When Ridge didn't continue, Gibby sighed again and said, "So, what? Are you a foreign exchange student or something? Do you come from a country that worships dumpsters and wears national uniforms?"

Ridge tugged the collar of his shirt. "This isn't a uniform. It's a holodrip, and it was really expensive. When my mom found out how many credits I spent on it, she—"

Gibby held up her hand. "Okay, okay, fine. It's expensive and mind-blowing and not at all weird and cultish. Get to the point."

"I don't know where to start, exactly," Ridge said.

"Start at the beginning," Michael suggested.

Ridge laughed. The sound broke through the courtyard.

"What's so funny?" Gibby said.

"It's just an ironic thing to say. 'Start at the beginning.'"

Michael wasn't sure what ironic meant. "Why?" he asked.

"It just is."

"Oh, who cares," Gibby said. "This conversation is played out." She gave Michael a look that said "Let's go." "But just so you know, Ridge—*master of the universe*. If you try to live on this bench, Mr. Ship's going to call the police."

"Who is Mr. Ship?" Ridge asked.

"The apartment manager." Gibby stood up. Michael did too. "Let's get out of here, Michael."

"Okay, okay, wait," Ridge said quickly, motioning for them to sit down. "I'll tell you where I'm from. You won't believe me, and it *might* destroy the entire space-time continuum as soon as I speak it into the universe, but I'll tell you, because I adhere to the Saeed Theory."

"The *what?*" Gibby said.

"The Saeed Theory. Saeed is a physicist in my timeline who says the fact that we continue to exist in our native timelines—and all other timelines, such as this one, for that matter—is proof that spatial teleportation is not as dangerous as people may believe, because obviously someone had to be the first to do it, and *obviously* everyone is still breathing and living—"

Gibby's hand was up again. "This is like having a conversation with the Riddler. Could you *please* get to the point and say something that actually makes *sense*? Even if it's just, like, a teeny-tiny morsel of sense?"

They stared at him, waiting, and after a long stretch of silence, in which all they heard was the distant drone of crickets, Gibby said, "Well? *Well?*"

Ridge closed his eyes, as if bracing for the news, even though he already knew what it was.

"I'm from the future," he said.

A **Spatial Teleportation Module (STM)** sends persons and/or objects to fixed moments in time (see *Timeprints*) through a process known as "energy conversion," during which the persons and/or objects are converted into dematerialized energy patterns and delivered to timeprints via subfrequency spatial transmitters.

Spatial teleportation requires access to an STM and possession of a handheld homing device known as the EGG. To initiate spatial teleportation, the traveler enters the STM with the EGG and designates their chosen timeprint. The EGG subsequently scans his/ her/their thumbprint on the EGG to trigger energy conversion. The STM will then deliver the scientist to the chosen timeprint at the same latitude and longitude as the STM.

Construction of the first STM prototype began in 2182 as a joint effort between the Global Science Council and the University of Delaware Spatial Sciences Department, led by Maria Sabio, PhD, DST, Chief STS, University of Delaware. The prototype was completed in 2199. It is housed in the Spatial Sciences Department at UD Red Knot.

From *The Encyclopedia Britannica-Barlowe*
(2199)

7

No one spoke for a long time.

"You think I'm delusional, don't you?" Ridge said.

That was exactly what Michael had been thinking.

"I know it's impossible to believe, but I'm telling the truth." Ridge's voice was even. He barely blinked. He looked like he was telling the truth, but that didn't mean anything. Maybe Ridge really did think he was from the future. That didn't make it so.

"Okay," Gibby said, shrugging. "Prove it."

"How?"

"Well." Gibby's lips scrunched up, the way they did when she was thinking. "Let's start with basic questions. What year are you from?"

"I shouldn't tell you that."

"Tell us how you got here, then," said Gibby.

"I shouldn't tell you that either."

Michael leaned forward. "Did you come here in a time machine or something?"

He hoped he sounded grown-up, even if it felt like a ridiculous question. Surely there were no such things as time machines.

"It's not called a time machine," Ridge said, his voice brighter. "It's an STM. Spatial Teleportation Module." He paused and studied their faces. "Have you ever heard of spatial teleportation?"

"No," Michael and Gibby said in unison.

"Oh," Ridge replied. "Well. Delaware is the capital of spatial teleportation. The scientific capital of the world, actually. The greatest scientists in the world live here, from on-world and off-world."

Michael's mind raced. There was too much strange information packed into those sentences. Delaware wasn't the capital of anything except tax-free shopping.

"What do you mean, on-world and off-world?" Gibby asked.

Ridge's face fell. He groaned and put his head in his hands. "This is a disaster. *I'm* a disaster. I'm probably causing the end of the world, like, right now. But I couldn't help it.

Shale goaded me. And it's 1999! The best year!" He leaned back against the bench. "The Backstreet Boys! Britney Spears! *Fight Club*! *The Matrix*! Ricky Martin, livin' la vida loca! I mean, yes, I was goaded, but the truth is, I *wanted* to see it. All of it. Especially the mall. Ordinary, everyday life. Word?"

Ridge was using words and sentences, sure, but Michael couldn't make sense of any of them. The best year? Shale? Goading? The Backstreet Boys?

"*What* the *heck* are you talking about?" Gibby blurted out. Except she didn't say heck. She used another word instead. "What is Shale? And how did it goad you? And what do the Backstreet Boys have to do with all this?"

"My brothers."

"The Backstreet Boys are your *brothers*?" Gibby said.

"No, no," Ridge said. "My brothers are the ones who goaded me. Well, my one brother, Shale. He kept saying I was all big talk. And I have no idea what's going to happen because no one has ever used the STM. I'm the first one," he said. His eyes suddenly snapped up like he'd just made a momentous discovery. "*I'm the first one.*"

"The first one what?" Michael asked.

Ridge's voice was breathless. "The first time traveler."

"Oh geez," Gibby said, crossing her arms.

Ridge glanced back and forth between them. "I promise I'm telling the truth. Don't you believe me?"

"Obviously not," Gibby said.

"I know, it sounds unbelievable. But I can prove it."

He reached into his back pocket and pulled out a book. It didn't look like a normal book, though. For one thing, it was small—small enough to fit in a back pocket, clearly. And it didn't have a title. "Wait . . . no." Ridge closed his eyes and said, under his breath, *"Don't be reckless, Ridge."*

He put the book away.

"What was that?" asked Michael.

"It's called a sumbook," Ridge said. "But it's too dangerous to open. I can't risk it. My mother would kill me. There must be another way."

Michael was suddenly desperate to see the book again. What did he mean, it was too dangerous to open? Would a bright, glowing light shine from its pages and burn their eyeballs out? Was there some secret spell written inside? Was—

"Maybe I could tell you something that's going to happen," Ridge said. "Something you can't change." He pursed his lips. His knee bopped up and down.

"No offense, but this is all a little cuckoo for my taste," Gibby said. "More than a little. I mean—"

"It's August seventeenth, right?" Ridge interrupted.

"Right," Michael said. *My birthday.*

"August seventeenth, 1999," Ridge mumbled. "August

seventeenth, 1999." His leg stopped moving. If there had been a light bulb over his head, it would have lit up. "There's going to be an earthquake tonight."

Michael sat up and gripped the bench. "Here?"

"No, no," Ridge said quickly. "Not here. In Turkey. No one knows it's going to happen, because you haven't developed a system to predict earthquakes yet. Earthquakes always hit without warning. It's going to strike around eight p.m. Delaware time. It'll be three a.m. there when it happens, with a magnitude of seven point six. The shaking will last for thirty-seven seconds." He looked at them. "But you can't tell anyone. Seriously. *No one.*"

"Oh please," Gibby said. She looked at Michael. "Don't listen to him. There's not going to be any earthquake."

"There will be," Ridge said. "And there's nothing anyone on this bench can do about it, so there can't be any harm in telling you. Right?"

AUDIO TRANSCRIPT

DATE
08/17/2199
LOCATION
SPATIAL TELEPORTATION SCIENCES DEPARTMENT
UNIVERSITY OF DELAWARE, RED KNOT CAMPUS
LABORATORY A2122

SUBJECTS

SABIO, MARIA (F/52YO/162CM/70KG/BRN/BRN/
IQ163), PHD, DST, CHIEF STS
SABIO, IAN (M/18YO/182CM/86KG/BRN/BRN/IQ157),
STUDENT
SABIO, SHALE (M/17YO/181CM/89KG/BLU/BRN/
IQ145), STUDENT
SABIO, RIDGE (M/16YO/172CM/73KG/BRN/BRN/
IQ160), STUDENT
SABIO, BEX (NB/14YO/148CM/46KG/BLU/BRN/
IQ158), STUDENT

SABIO, MARIA:
I have to meet with the dean. It'll take
about fifteen minutes. Study the sumbook
while I'm gone. We'll discuss Hurricane Floyd
when I get back.

SABIO, BEX:
Can we use our Keplars just for today?

SABIO, MARIA:
How many times do I have to say no? You need
to get accustomed to the sumbooks. All of
you. You need technology that makes sense in
any timeprint.

SABIO, BEX:
Ugh. We know, we know. They're just . . .
bulky.

SABIO, MARIA:
If you know, then why do I have to keep
repeating myself?

SABIO, IAN:
Go to your meeting, Mom. I'll make sure they
keep their eyes on their sumbooks.

SABIO, MARIA:
I'll be back in fifteen minutes.

//EXIT SABIO, MARIA VIA WEST DOOR

SABIO, BEX:
You're so spurious, Ian. It's embarrassing.

SABIO, IAN:
It got her to stop talking, didn't it?

SABIO, BEX:
True.

SABIO, SHALE:
Did any of you see Hammond's face during the
demo this morning? He was so jealous of my
GSC pin. He really thought he was going to
get it. I should bombard him with holos. Just
one holo after another. Me and the pin at the
park. Me and the pin at the pond. Me and the
pin taking a walk. His face when he walked in
and saw it!

SABIO, RIDGE:
Maybe he was wondering why you wore your pin
to an STM demo when there was absolutely no
reason to.

SABIO, SHALE:
Why shouldn't I? I want everyone to know I
got it. It sends a message.

SABIO, RIDGE:
Yeah. The message is, you're annoying.

SABIO, SHALE:
What's wrong with being proud of your
accomplishments? Especially if they come with
awards.

SABIO, RIDGE:
You can be proud without being annoying.

SABIO, SHALE:
Ha! What do you know about it? You've never
won anything. Highest IQ, and for what?
Nothing.

SABIO, RIDGE:
That's not true. I use my IQ—my *genius-
level* IQ—for lots of things. For example,
last night I ported to Aderlaine Giverny's
house so we could go star watching on the
riverfront.

SABIO, SHALE:
You did *not*. How did you do it, without Mom
catching you?

SABIO, RIDGE:
I told you. I used my genius-level IQ. You
might have gold pins, but I'm having *fun*.
Remember that twentieth-century poet we
studied? "Tell me, what is it you plan to do
with your one wild and precious life?" Well,
I do *not* plan on wasting it in this lab, day
after day after day, learning how to become
spatial teleportation scientists. Especially
when spatial teleportation may never actually
happen.

SABIO, BEX:
[GASP.] You think it's not possible?

SABIO, RIDGE:
I didn't say that. In fact, I have no doubt
it *is* possible. But that doesn't mean it's
going to happen. Mom and the other GSC
members are too wrapped up in the unknowns.
What if it destroys the space-time continuum?
What if the universe ceases to exist? What
if spatial sickness is a real thing? Waaah
waaah waaah. They're all too scared to
actually *do* something. They'll never know
until someone tries it. But like I said,
they're too scared. Especially that prune Dr.
Jameson. Instead, we talk about it day after
day after day, learning to be obedient little
scientists, as if we're on a holo loop. And
not a good one, either. If I hear Dr. Jameson
mention spatial sickness one more time—

SABIO, IAN:
So, did you kiss or what?

SABIO, RIDGE:
Me and Dr. Jameson?

SABIO, IAN:
No, cretin. You and Aderlaine.

SABIO, RIDGE:
Well. No. Not exactly.

SABIO, SHALE:
What do you mean, not exactly?

SABIO, RIDGE:
She didn't want to go to the riverfront. She
said she had homework.

SABIO, SHALE:
Ha!

SABIO, IAN:
She chose *homework* over you, then?

SABIO, RIDGE:
She has a lot of studying to do! She's very
studious!

SABIO, BEX:
Can we stop talking about ridiculous things
like kisses and prunes and get back to the
sumbooks? Mom said—

SABIO, RIDGE:
Ugh! Mom said, Mom said. It's as if Mom rules
our entire lives.

SABIO, SHALE:
That's because she *does* rule our entire
lives.

SABIO, RIDGE:
If I oversaw this operation, there would be
spatial teleporters in every timeprint—

SABIO, IAN:
Destroying the universe.

SABIO, RIDGE:
—*learning* and *investigating* and—

SABIO, IAN:
Destroying the universe.

SABIO, RIDGE:
Spatial teleportation isn't as dangerous as
people say. Think about it. More than likely,
people have already done it, and that's
what got us to where we are right now—this
sterile, boring, overly monitored lab.

SABIO, SHALE:
You're all talk. If you had the opportunity
right now to use the STM, you wouldn't get
in. You'd be too afraid. Remember when you
were three and you cried because a drone hurt
your feelings? Ha!

SABIO, RIDGE:
I was *three*.

SABIO, BEX:
Can we *please* get back to—

SABIO, SHALE:
You're all talk, Ridge. Always have been.
What do you think, Ian? Do you think Ridge
would seriously get in the STM if he had the
chance? Without anyone giving it a test run
ahead of time?

SABIO, IAN:
Maybe. He *is* incredibly reckless for someone
with a high IQ.

SABIO, RIDGE:
Genius IQ.

SABIO, SHALE:
If that number is even accurate.

SABIO, RIDGE:
What's that supposed to mean?

SABIO, SHALE:
There are upgrade credits for that sort of
thing. That's all I'm saying.

SABIO, RIDGE:
I would never use upgrade credits for my
intelligence quotient. I don't *need* to. Maybe
you should consider it, though.

SABIO, IAN:
Let's not start a—

SABIO, SHALE:
I don't need it! I don't need *any* upgrades!
You're nothing but a reckless, arrogant
cretin with a *suspiciously high* IQ!

SABIO, BEX:
Can we not—

SABIO, IAN:
Let's return to the sumbook. Mom will be back
any second, and if we don't know anything
about Hurricane Floyd, she's going to make
us recite every international election and
natural disaster from memory.

SABIO, RIDGE:
Thankfully, my memory is eidetic. And I don't
need pins to prove it.

SABIO, SHALE:
You're insufferable!

SABIO, RIDGE:
Insufferable with an eidetic memory and a
genius IQ—

SABIO, IAN:
Enough! Let's focus. Pretend it's September
1999. You've just teleported into the
aftermath of Hurricane Floyd. What do you
see?

SABIO, SHALE:
I can tell you what Ridge sees. His massive
ego with nothing to back it up.

SABIO, RIDGE:
You ignorant—

SABIO, IAN:
This is a tired discussion. And now is not the time.

SABIO, SHALE:
Now *is* the time. He almost destroyed the
entire STM demo today with his big talk. Mom
is always telling him not to be reckless, but
what she really means is not to be stupid. He
acts like he's some big—

SABIO, BEX:
Can we get back to the sumbooks, please?

SABIO, SHALE:
—important science genius, but all he does is
talk! He never does anything worthwhile! He
thinks he doesn't have to work hard because
of his so-called genius-level IQ! All he does
is sit around and listen to ancient music
and pretend like he's already a disciplined
scientist with the GSC!

SABIO, IAN:
I know he can be frustrating, but so can you.
For that matter, so can Bex.

SABIO, BEX:
Hey, what did I do? Why are you bringing me
into this?

SABIO, IAN:
Everyone, please sit down before Mom gets
back.

SABIO, BEX:
In what ways am I frustrating? From my
estimations, that's highly unlikely. Name
three ways I'm frustrating. No, four. In
order, from most frustrating to least—

SABIO, SHALE:
This! *This* is why you're frustrating, Bex!

SABIO, IAN:
Everyone, please—

SABIO, BEX:
All I said was to list my most frustrating characteristics in order from most frustrating to least frustrating.

SABIO, SHALE:
Okay. You want a list? I'll start one right now, Bex. Number one—THIS CONVERSATION. Number two—*this conversation.* Number three? This—

SABIO, IAN:
Okay. Point made. Now can we *please*—

SABIO, BEX:
Wait. Where is Ridge? [PAUSE.] Did anyone see him leave?

SABIO, IAN:
He must have gone to the back.

SABIO, BEX:
Why would he—

SABIO, IAN:
Oh no.

SABIO, BEX:
You don't think . . .

SABIO, IAN:
Wait, wait, wait—

SABIO, BEX:
Ridge!

SABIO, IAN:
Holosecurity, put a hold on Ridge Sabio!

HOLOSECURITY:
Prepare for hold on subject Ridge Sabio.

//HOLD INITIATED
//HOLD UNSUCCESSFUL

HOLOSECURITY:
Subject is in a protected location.

//STM1 TIMEPRINT ENTERED 08171999
//STM1 TIMEPRINT ACCEPTED 08171999

SABIO, IAN:
Oh no.

SABIO, BEX:
Mom is going to be so mad.

SABIO, SHALE:
I told you he was reckless!

SABIO, IAN:
Ridge, get out of there! You don't know what
you're doing! What if you rematerialize
inside a building or a tree? Think about
this! Imagine being crushed by concrete or
suffocating inside a tree trunk!

SABIO, BEX:
Do something, Ian!

SABIO, IAN:
I'm trying! He's inside and it's all powered
up because of the demo!

SABIO, SHALE: This is exactly the kind of
thing I'm talking about! He's irresponsible!
Reckless! And now look! Only an idiot would—

//EXIT SABIO, RIDGE VIA STM1
//STM1 MALFUNCTION
//STM1 AUTO-INITIATING
//STM1 MALFUNCTION

SABIO, BEX:
He's gone! He's gone!

SABIO, IAN:
Mom is going to be so mad.

SABIO, BEX:
What's the timeprint? Where did he go?

SABIO, IAN:
I don't know, I don't know!

SABIO, SHALE:
What do you mean, you don't know?

SABIO, IAN:
All the readouts are blank. I don't know what
happened. I don't know. Get Mom! Get Mom!

SABIO, SHALE:
Holosecurity, emergency transport Dr. Sabio to present location!

HOLOSECURITY:
Passcode required for emergency teleportation of subject Dr. Maria Sabio.

SABIO, BEX:
Did you see anything before the timeprint went out?

SABIO, IAN:
No. Just a bunch of numbers. I don't remember any of them. Maybe an eight? And a bunch of nines? We need Mom. We need Mom!

SABIO, BEX:
See? I am definitely *not* the most frustrating person in this family.

8

A row of shoes sat obediently by the door of the Rosarios' apartment. "No shoes in the house" was one of Ms. Rosario's firm rules, along with "Pick up after yourself" and "Never go to bed angry," but when Michael came in, his mother smiled at him from the couch and said he could keep his Jordans on if he wanted, which he did. Her wet hair was wrapped in a towel that had once been bright yellow but had faded into a sad pastel.

He went to the couch and sat down as his mother picked up the remote.

"You all right, hon?" she said. "You have a weird look on your face." She glanced toward the door. "Did someone say something to you out there?"

Ever since they'd moved into the apartment complex earlier that year, she'd been worried that they'd have a repeat of sixth grade, when some of the kids gave Michael a hard time about his clothes, the way he always wanted to help the teachers, how he barely spoke when he had to give reports in front of the class. At his old school, he sat alone at lunch. Sometimes he'd bring a book from the library, even though he didn't like to read. He just wanted to look like he was doing something.

"New school district, new apartment, new beginnings," his mother had said when they moved in.

"If we survive Y2K," Michael had added.

"I was talking to Gibby, that's all," Michael said. He looked at the clock. It was seven thirty. "Everything's fine. We were just trying to figure something out."

"What did you need to figure out?"

"Something with her dad." He hated lying, especially to his mother, but he knew this was the quickest way to change the subject. His mother despised Mr. Gibson. So did Michael. Gibby didn't like him much either. Michael suspected that the reason Gibby had offered to babysit in the first place was that her father was the reason Michael's mom lost her job. Mr. Gibson had been Ms. Rosario's boss.

"Tsk," his mother said. "That man."

She turned on the television. *Wheel of Fortune* was just getting started.

Michael stared blankly at the screen. He pushed his thumb into the palm of his hand. He glanced at the clock.

Where was Turkey, anyway? Last year, during a geography lesson, he'd had to fill in the state names on a blank map of the United States and he couldn't even do that. Forget knowing the rest of the world. Was Turkey in Asia? Europe? Africa? How many people lived there? What kinds of food did they eat? What language did they speak?

He swallowed. Brought both hands together and clenched them into a tight fist on his lap.

What were people in Turkey doing right now? Were they sleeping? Laughing? Dancing? Watching game shows on the couch with their mothers?

Michael felt a familiar burn behind his eyes, the one that meant tears were forming. No, no, no. If he cried, his mother would want to know why, especially because it was his birthday, and he wouldn't be able to lie, and then she would worry, and besides, the whole thing was ridiculous, wasn't it? Ridge was out of his mind. He had to be. Time travel wasn't real. Everyone knew that.

But his heart pounded anyway.

"I think I would be good on *Wheel of Fortune*," his mother said.

It was 7:37.

"Where's Turkey?" Michael blurted without thinking.

His mother turned to him. "What?"

"Turkey."

"The country?"

He nodded.

"It's in the Middle East," she said. "Near Syria and . . ." She paused, thinking. "Greece, I think. Why?"

Michael swallowed. "Just wondering. No reason."

What if an earthquake really was coming? What if it was true and he was one of the only people who knew about it? If Ridge was right, if an earthquake was on its way, shouldn't they tell someone?

But how? How do you warn an entire country that something terrible is about to happen?

Michael's stomach knotted and rolled.

"I'm gonna make some popcorn," his mother said, standing. "You want some?"

He had to do something, didn't he? He eyed the phone on the kitchen counter. He could make a long-distance call, maybe. But he didn't know how. And he didn't know who to call in the first place. Maybe he could call Mr. Mosley. He would know what to do, wouldn't he?

Maybe he could ask his mama for help.

But how would he explain it? What if it destroyed the "space-time continuum," whatever that meant? Besides, his mother looked so tired, even right now, as she placed a bag of popcorn in the microwave. She had so many worries. He didn't want to add to them. That's why he was the one stockpiling for Y2K, so she wouldn't have to worry.

He wished he'd never gone outside to talk to Ridge. He wished there was a way to forget the things you knew. He wished, he wished, he wished.

At 7:47, his mother switched away from a commercial to Channel Five. *Guinness World Records* would come on at eight. A man was going to balance a motorcycle on his teeth. Michael's knee bounced up and down, up and down, up and down.

"You're shaking the whole couch," his mother said. "Are you sure everything's okay?"

"Yes, Mom," Michael said. He cleared his throat. "It's just weird, isn't it? Balancing a motorcycle on your teeth? Doesn't make sense."

"Sometimes things don't make sense," his mother said. "Especially the strangest things."

Ten minutes later, his mother took the towel off her head and wandered off to drop it in the laundry. She came back brushing her hair. It was still damp and smelled like the same dollar-store shampoo that Michael used.

"Are the shoes comfortable?" she asked, eyes on his shiny new shoes.

"Yep," he replied, eyes on the tired old clock.

Three minutes later, Michael pushed his sneakers deep into the carpet. He could practically *feel* the ground shake beneath him. He didn't, of course; there were oceans and continents between Delaware and Turkey, but he imagined how it would all unfold. He looked around his apartment—empty water glasses on the kitchen counter, school pictures on the wall, the fake plants his mother put near the door to give the apartment some life—and saw them all trembling, tumbling, breaking, falling into a crack in the earth, and then he asked himself what he would do if an earthquake hit right now, would he be strong enough to save his mother, would he shield her with his body, was his body even big enough to shield anyone? What could a boy like him do, a boy who did nothing and knew nothing? But the trouble was, he *did* know something. He knew that somewhere far away, a terrible thing was happening to someone just like him, someone with pictures on the wall and new sneakers and birthdays and a mama.

"Michael," his mother said, lowering her brush to her lap. "Tell me what's wrong."

He looked at her. "Nothing, Mom. I promise."

"Then why are you crying?"

Was he? Oh no—was he? When had that happened? Boys weren't supposed to cry, this much he knew. Not even in front of their mamas. That's something babies did. Little boys. Not men. Beejee had probably never cried in his whole life.

Michael blinked. That's when the tear fell, warm on his cheek. He wiped it away with his shoulder.

"I'm just happy about my birthday, that's all."

"Oh, my little boy," she said. She kissed his forehead. "My sweet, perfect boy."

9

"Maybe it didn't happen," Michael said that night, to the water stain. It was just before ten p.m. His mother had gone to bed, so Michael went to bed too. His sneakers were lined up by the door, but he was still fully dressed, lying on top of his covers with the cordless phone on his chest, just in case he decided to call Mr. Mosley after all. "Maybe it didn't happen," he repeated.

Then the phone rang, and Gibby was on the other end.

"It happened," she said. "The thing he told us. I just saw it on the news."

A thousand images raced through Michael's mind, all of them horrifying.

"Oh," he said.

"There's no way he could have known what would happen, right?" Gibby said, her voice low. "Unless he was telling the truth?"

Funnily enough, Michael hadn't really thought about Ridge until this moment. He was so focused on the earthquake. All those people.

"Was anyone hurt?" Michael asked. "Did it say on the news?"

Gibby paused. "They don't know how many, exactly."

"I bet it was a lot," Michael said. He cleared his throat. "I mean, an earthquake that big."

"It'll probably be in the papers tomorrow," Gibby said.

"Yeah."

"I don't know what to think about this whole situation, but I'll figure it out." She switched into babysitter voice. The one that said, "You're a child, but if you listen to me, all your troubles will go away." Even though they never did. "Don't worry, okay? And don't talk to anyone about this. You can keep a secret, right?"

Michael hated when she talked to him like he was a kid who didn't know how to do anything. Even though that was exactly what he felt like at this moment.

"Yes," he said. "Okay."

He hung up and stared at the ceiling.

"I'm not a little boy," he said.

NPR DOUBLETALK GLOBALCAST

CASTDATE: 01/07/2199

DASHKA MEDINA, HOST:

Welcome to *NPR Doubletalk Globalcast*, an open forum to discuss controversial issues of the day with the world's leading minds. This evening, we're shining a light on one of the most talked-about scientific developments in modern history— potentially, in all of history—the completion of the first Spatial Teleportation Module, or STM, colloquially known as a "time machine." The unveiling of the STM and the planned demo, scheduled to take place later this year, has ignited fervor across the globe. Here to discuss the varied points of view are Dr. Maria Sabio, lead spatial teleportation scientist and head engineer of the STM project at the University of Delaware; Dr. Eliot Jameson, epidemiologist with Johns Hopkins University; and Drs. Case Robinson, Anna Botha, and Dola Adebayo, physicists with the Massachusetts Institute of Technology, Stanford University, and Caltech, respectively.

Welcome, everyone, for what promises to be a lively discussion. Let's kick this off with Dr. Sabio, who, along with her team, unveiled the STM at the University of Delaware Red Knot campus. The University of Delaware has taken a leading role in the evolution of spatial teleportation sciences, with Dr. Sabio at the helm. The NPR science team has done extensive coverage on the history of the STM and the growing field of spatial teleportation.

[HOLOHOST: Doubleblink to view related coverage.]
Thanks for being here, Dr. Sabio.

DR. SABIO:

Thanks for having me.

MEDINA:

There have been polarizing reactions to the unveiling of the STM. On one side, there's a palpable level of excitement about the new possibilities offered by spatial teleportation. On the other, there is outrage at the entire concept. Some of that outrage has been expressed by members of this panel, in fact. Can you share your thoughts on these polarizing responses?

DR. SABIO:

I have nothing but respect for my fellow scientists. I understand their concerns. I hope to put their minds at ease by reiterating our position at UD: we don't plan to use the STM until we're certain it's safe and in service to the global good. We don't—

DR. BOTHA:

Unfortunately, there's no way for us to know what is or is not for the global good until someone actually teleports, which could, theoretically, destroy life as we know it. I don't understand how Dr. Sabio can be so casual about such a risk.

DR. SABIO:

It's not my intention to come off as casual. I just—

DR. ROBINSON:

Dr. Botha is exactly right. That's the problem with this entire field of science. Such a module should have never been built in the first place, in my opinion.

MEDINA:

Can you expound on that, Dr. Robinson?

DR. ROBINSON:

No good can come from it. If we start manipulating historical events, where does that lead? Where does it end? Are we going to travel back in time and prevent genocide, world wars, the atomic bomb? How exactly would that work? The fact is, history is populated by humans, and humans are deeply flawed and imperfect, and no amount of spatial teleportation can correct that.

DR. SABIO:

It's not our intention to correct the mistakes of the past, Dr. Robinson. As I've said many, *many* times, my vision is historical research. If the GSC ever gives the green light for us to put the STM to use—which we wouldn't do until we've completed all safety protocols—we would send trained scientists to their preselected timeprints with clear orders of what they can or cannot do. No decent scientist would interfere with—

DR. ROBINSON:

Last I checked, scientists were humans, and let me say again— humans are deeply flawed and imperfect, and no amount of training or orders can correct that.

DR. ADEBAYO:

In Dr. Sabio's defense, there are other options. Caltech is currently developing alternatives. Research can be conducted by AI, for example, instead of humans.

DR. JAMESON:

That's the only way to mitigate some of the risks.

MEDINA:

Thanks for chiming in, Dr. Jameson. As I mentioned at the opening of the program, you're an epidemiologist with Johns Hopkins, in contrast with our other guests, who are physicists. Can you tell our audience what your stake is in all this?

DR. JAMESON:

I work as an adviser to the Global Science Council. My specific focus is on infectious diseases and their role in spatial teleportation.

MEDINA:

Can you explain?

DR. JAMESON:

There are ethical, moral, even legal implications to traveling to other timeprints. But there are also significant health risks. Not just the risks of dematerialization and rematerialization, but the risks of contracting and transmitting infectious diseases from one timeprint to another.

MEDINA:

Such as?

DR. JAMESON:

We've eradicated many of the diseases that have plagued humankind. We have revolutionary health tools like the HUCK that can provide immediate diagnosis, treatment, sometimes *cures* in a matter of minutes. But the HUCK is not designed to combat every infection or disease in history, especially those that are deeply complex, such as the AIDS virus or the Black Death. Moreover, a spatial teleportation scientist from the twenty-second century is not immune or protected against infections of the past. Scientists from 2199 could die from an ordinary illness in another timeprint, for example, because they have no immunity against it. A person could travel to 1950, only to die of the chicken pox. That's why it makes more sense to send AI instead of humans.

DR. SABIO:

This is why UD works so closely with Dr. Jameson,, as well as the team at Caltech and the Centers for Disease Control. We want to determine if there is a way to inoculate scientists with a single vaccine that would protect them from—

DR. ROBINSON:

Is that *really* the best use of resources?

DR. ADEBAYO:

Dr. Robinson, you're a scientist. Are you not committed to pushing the limits of science? Do you not see the value in research and development that could further—

DR. ROBINSON:

I'm committed to pushing the limits of science in areas that don't threaten the lives of everyone on this panel and everyone watching at home. That's what I'm committed to.

DR. BOTHA:

I have to agree with Dr. Robinson. Just because science *can* do something doesn't mean it *should*.

MEDINA:

Dr. Sabio, do you have anything to say in response?

DR. SABIO:

As I stated earlier, I understand the concerns of all my colleagues. I want to reassure everyone here, and everyone watching, that there are no immediate plans to send anyone or anything to another timeprint. It will be at least five to ten years before that's a safe consideration, perhaps even longer. To do so any sooner would be incredibly irresponsible.

10

They found Ridge on the bench the next morning. His eyes were heavy and dark, like he could fall asleep at any moment. Michael knew that look; his mother wore it often.

"No one called the police," Ridge said as they sat next to him. "I maxed and relaxed here all night."

"Maxed and relaxed?" Gibby said.

"That's what people say, right? Maxing and relaxing? I've been studying the late nineties for months—"

"Look," Gibby interrupted. "I don't know what's going on, but you predicted an earthquake halfway around the world, and I want to know how."

"I didn't *predict* it," Ridge clarified. "It happened two hundred years ago."

Michael's eyes widened into saucers. "Two hundred years?"

Ridge cursed under his breath. "My mom is going to *have a cow* when she finds out what I've done. What I'm doing. What I did. Not just one cow. Probably an entire herd."

Gibby pinched the bridge of her nose. "You might consider pulling back on the slang."

"How else will I fit in?"

She glanced at him. "You're not exactly fitting in. I mean. Look at your clothes."

"I told you, this was incredibly expensive. And *of course* my clothes don't make sense in *this* timeprint. But where I'm from, this is projecting holoimages. Any ones I want. If you had adequate technology, you'd see it. Besides, I have nothing else to wear," Ridge continued. "I left unexpectedly."

Michael stood up. He wasn't in the mood to talk about clothes or holoimages or whatever. He was still thinking about the earthquake. All those people.

"If you're from the future, tell us what happens with Y2K," he said, surprised by the edge in his voice. "Is it all going to end on January first?"

Ridge's eyebrows knotted together. "Is *what* going to end?"

"Civilization as we know it," said Michael.

Gibby stood up too. She put her hand on Michael's

shoulder. But he didn't want it there. He wanted to shake it off, push it away. *I'm not a kid.*

Ridge looked up at both of them.

"Well?" Michael said. "What's going to happen?"

"I'm sorry, Mike, but I can't tell you—"

"It's Michael! *Michael*. Not Mike." A flame of frustration gathered in Michael's chest and roared to life. "And why can't you tell us? You told us all about that earthquake."

"That's different. There was nothing you could do."

Michael raised his arms and dropped them to his sides. "Exactly!"

"Michael—" Gibby began.

"I wouldn't have traveled here if it was a dangerous time to be alive," Ridge said.

"It's always a dangerous time to be alive," Michael said. "Depending on who and where you are."

Ridge paused. "You're right. But this moment, right now? The three of us at Fox Run Apartments in north Delaware in 1999? It's not one of those dangerous times."

"That's easy for you to say," Michael said.

Gibby took her hand off Michael's shoulder. "Michael's right," she said. "You expect us to trust you, but you won't answer any of our questions."

"I know I'm asking you to believe something unbelievable," Ridge said. "But the truth is, I need your help, whether you believe me or not. There's no way my mom will *ever* let me become a spatial teleportation scientist after this. I'll probably become a prisoner in my own room—*if* she doesn't kill me as soon as I rematerialize."

"So?" Gibby said.

"*So* . . . I can only stay here a short time. I know I won't be able see all the things I want to see, but . . ."

When no one said anything, Ridge continued.

"There's one thing that I really want to do, one thing I *really* want to see. Something I've read about. A place filled with contemporary sights and sounds and teenagers and everyday, ordinary life. A place where you can get anything you need in the 1990s and find all kinds of things you didn't *know* you needed. A place where people shop in real life, in real places," he said. He smiled. Slow, friendly, warm. "I want to go to the mall."

Indoor shopping centers with one or more anchor stores were known as shopping malls, or malls. The popularity of malls gained significant momentum during this period, peaking in 1992. As the 2000s progressed, however, consumer habits shifted away from department stores and malls, which triggered their eventual decline.

Malls were a popular meeting place for American teenagers, particularly in the 1980s and 1990s. They were a center point for nineties pop culture, as detailed in the *Pop Culture Omnibus (1990–2020)*.

Christiana Mall in Newark, Delaware, was the last American mall to close its doors. Its final day of operation was February 17, 2052.

Excerpt from The Spatial Teleportation Summary Book for the Turn of the Twenty-First Century (1980–2020), *compiled by Maria Sabio, PhD, DST, Chief STS, University of Delaware, translated from Original Eaker Linton Code*

11

It was strange, going into someone else's home. It was like learning a secret about them. Or, in the case of Gibby's apartment, being presented with an equation that didn't quite make sense. That's how Michael felt every time he walked through her door—like she didn't belong there.

He suspected she felt the same way.

Mismatched furniture, *MotorTrend* magazines, and remote controls crowded the living room. The walls were bare except for a single cheap clock that hung off-center on the wall next to the television, like it was counting down the minutes until you disappeared into a pit of despair. In the kitchen: a sink filled with dishes, because Mr. Gibson insisted that Gibby should do all the housework and she resisted until she could no longer tolerate the mess. Gibby once joked that she resented her mother for abandoning the family. Not because she loved her mother, but because she left Gibby with all the chores that her father and brother thought they were too manly to complete.

That was something Michael and Gibby had in common. Each had a parent who couldn't be bothered.

At least Michael had his mama, though.

When Michael and Gibby walked in, Beejee was leaning against the refrigerator, eating a slice of cold pizza.

"What're you doin' here?" Beejee asked.

They'd left Ridge at the bench. "Stay here, don't move," Gibby had said, like Ridge was a puppy.

"I live here, remember?" Gibby said. Her apartment had a similar layout to the Rosarios, but it was slightly bigger. More space around the kitchen. "What are *you* doing there? You have your own hovel now. I thought it was supposed to be your so-called bachelor pad."

Beejee held up the pizza. "Came here to eat breakfast before work," he said, mouth crammed with food. "Aren't you supposed to be *babysitting* at little Mikey's? Or did he want to borrow some of your dolls?" Beejee laughed.

Michael's feelings would have been hurt, but Beejee was such an idiot that Michael didn't care much about the doll comment. Instead, he wished he was bigger. Wide-shouldered and beefy, like Beejee, so he could shove him against the fridge and maybe punch him in the nose.

Not that he would.

But it would be nice to have the option.

"Actually, I was wondering if you had some clothes I could borrow that don't smell completely like a desecrated pig," Gibby said.

Beejee shrugged and shoved the last bits of crust into his mouth. "I don't know. Look in my old closet." He nodded toward Michael. "They won't fit this pipsqueak, though."

"They're not for Michael," said Gibby. "They're for a friend of mine who's going through a bad time. Can I look or what?" She was already halfway down the hall with Michael at her heels.

"Take whatever you want, but leave ten bucks on the counter!" Beejee called after them. "*At least* ten bucks!"

Gibby muttered something under her breath as Beejee left, slamming the apartment door behind him, but Michael couldn't hear what she said.

Minutes later, Gibby was rifling through the recesses of Beejee's disgusting closet, as Michael looked around his disgusting room—unmade bed with funky-smelling sheets, posters of women in bikinis, a small tower of empty Coca-Cola cans that had been there for who knows how long.

"My dad says he's going to make this into an office,"

Gibby said as she cobbled together a makeshift wardrobe of cargo pants, wrinkled shorts, and a few T-shirts. Michael followed her into the kitchen, where she stuffed it all into a plastic bag. "An office for what? All he does is come home and watch TV until he falls asleep in a puddle of his own drool."

Michael wanted to make a joke—there was something funny about what Gibby had said—but nothing came to him.

His mind never seemed to work when he needed it most.

They saw Mr. Mosley in front of Building L on their way back to the courtyard. The folds of his skin looked deeper than usual, and his smile seemed forced, like he was grinning through a grimace. He was wearing a faded Wilmington Blue Rocks shirt and jeans instead of his usual work clothes.

Michael frowned. "You all right, Mr. Mosley?"

"Yeah, I'm all right," he said. "I must have pulled a muscle painting that apartment. Told Ship I'd have to take the day off. Haven't called out sick once in four years, but man, this hurts something awful." He rubbed his arm. "I'm gonna go bored out of my mind laying around all day, but you gotta take care of your health when that's all you've got. Remember that."

Gibby's eyes lit up. "If you're going to sit at home all day, it's the perfect opportunity to read that book! I finished it last night. I never saw the ending coming. You'll love it, I promise!" Gibby shoved the bag of clothes toward Michael. "I'll go get it. Be right back!"

"You don't have to—" Mosley began. But Gibby was already off. Mosley sighed and motioned toward the bag. "What you got there?"

"Clothes for that guy. Ridge," said Michael.

"Why's he need clothes? Is he living on the streets?"

"No, no, not exactly," Michael said. "He just . . . doesn't have a place to live at the moment."

"So he's living on the streets."

"It's temporary," Michael said. The last thing they needed was for Mosley to call in reinforcements. "He got into an argument with his . . . uh, his stepdad, I think? And he just needed to get out of there for a while."

"Well. He can't sleep on the bench. Ship will call the cops." Mosley glanced back toward the manager's office. "Maybe we should find him a shelter or—"

"We're finding him a place," Michael said quickly. He cleared his throat.

Mosley paused, as if considering this. "What a shame, kid being on his own like that, even just for a couple days." He stretched his neck. His voice sounded far away. "My pop wasn't so great either. There were days when I would've been better off sleeping on a bench too." His eyes softened. "I was lucky, though. I had a good mama, like you. She'd take out money from every paycheck and drop it in a big jar with my name on it. When I left home for good, she gave the jar to me, and told me I'd been a good boy."

Michael's eyes widened, imagining an enormous jar full of cash. "You must have been rich!" he said.

Mosley laughed. "Nah. My mom worked at a diner. It was only a few hundred bucks." He rubbed his shoulder again and lowered his voice. "Don't look now, but here comes a bookworm."

Michael turned, and sure enough, Gibby was hurrying through the grass, waving her Christopher Pike book in the air.

Mosley shook his head. "What have I gotten myself into?" he said. "Now I have to read a book."

When the bench came into view, Gibby immediately started muttering, "Oh no, oh no, oh no," because Ridge was surrounded by the Prince brothers, presumably on their way to the basketball court, since Elijah had a basketball tucked under his arm.

They were all laughing, though, so apparently Ridge hadn't said anything that sounded completely delusional.

"Hey, Gibby," Jamar said. His smile took up half his face. "We just met your friend Ridge."

Elijah, the one who was Michael's age, said, "He told us

he was maxing and relaxing." He laughed good-naturedly.

The youngest brother, Darius, didn't say a word. He was standing next to Jamar and eyeing Ridge's clothes. Darius looked small and delicate next to his oldest brother.

Elijah tossed the basketball lightly in the air, caught it, then said, "Hey, nice Jordans!"

Michael looked down at his sneakers like he was seeing them for the first time.

"You wanna play some ball with us, Michael?" Jamar asked.

"Um . . . ," Michael said quietly. "I don't think so."

He was only slightly taller than Darius, who was four years younger.

How come everyone grew but him?

"You should go, Michael," Gibby said brightly. "Ridge and I can take care of . . . uh, the stuff we need to do."

Michael didn't really play basketball, but there was a secret part of him that suspected he might be good at it. His dad had played, after all. Maybe he'd inherited an athletic gene and didn't even know it.

Then again, his father had abandoned them before Michael even got to kindergarten, so perhaps it was best not to have inherited anything.

"Maybe another time," Michael said, but Jamar had started talking and no one heard him.

"How about you, Gibs?" Jamar was saying. He was smiling at Gibby again. Or maybe he'd never stopped smiling at her. Michael wasn't sure. "You ready for some one-on-one? Dunking contest, maybe?"

Gibby put her hand on her hips and giggled.

She *giggled*.

"Very funny, Mr. Sarcastic," she said.

Michael cleared his throat. "I'll play another time, okay?"

Jamar shrugged. "No problem. We'll be around." He headed toward the basketball court with Darius at his heels. Elijah trailed behind, spinning the ball in his hands.

"When you play, we'll have four," Elijah said to Michael as they walked away. "It's better with four."

Michael, Gibby, and Ridge watched the Prince brothers disappear behind one of the buildings. Then Gibby took the bag of clothes from Michael and tossed them on Ridge's lap.

"I got you some clothes so you don't look like a total maniac, though I'm not sure it'll help much if you go around telling people you're maxing and relaxing," Gibby said. "Now if you want our help—if you want us to take you to the *mall*, of all places—you *have to* tell us something. Give us some nugget of information."

"Okay," Ridge said. "I'll show you how I got here. But we have to go someplace private, where no one will see us."

"Fine," Gibby said. "We'll go to Michael's."

"What if Mr. Mosley stops by for lunch?" Michael asked. "Or earlier, since he's home sick today?"

"Well, we can't go to my house," Gibby said. "I don't know which shift my dad's working, and if he finds me at home with a guy . . ."

"I don't know if it's a good idea anyway," Michael said.

What if Ridge wanted to get them alone so he could murder them? Sure, he didn't *look* like a murderer, but then again, who did?

It didn't matter, though, because no one was listening to Michael. Instead, Gibby reached into her pocket and pulled out her keys. "I know where we can go," she said. "But you're not gonna like it."

12

If Gibby's apartment was an equation that didn't quite make sense, Beejee's was a perfect sum. Michael had never been there before, but he had an idea what it probably looked like, and that was exactly what it turned out to be. The couch was tattered and stained, with stuffing poking out of the cushions. There was a faint smell of dirty socks, which emanated from a pair of sneakers next to the front door. The place was dotted with milk crates being used as shelves and containers—four by the television, packed with DVDs and CDs; one sitting on top of the kitchen counter, half filled with tools; and another by the couch with magazines. Mostly muscle car magazines, it looked like.

"Is it okay that we're here?" Michael asked. He imagined

Beejee in a fiery rage, storming in and demanding to know what they were doing in his apartment.

Gibby sat on the couch and shrugged. "He gave me a key for emergencies, and this is an emergency." She swept her arm toward Ridge, who was coming to sit next to her. "You said you'd explain everything if we were someplace private. Well, here we are. Someplace private."

Michael remained by the door. His eyes drifted toward the kitchen. The refrigerator. The open box of Cocoa Puffs on the counter. The milk crate and its tools.

"Come sit down, Michael," Gibby said. "Don't worry. Beejee's at work. He won't be home for hours."

He hated that she thought he was afraid of Beejee.

He hated that she was right.

He went to the couch, sat down. He smelled the faint scent of Gibby's strawberry shampoo, mixed with a tinge of body odor from Ridge—he hadn't showered, after all—and the unplaceable odor that was, no doubt, Beejee.

"Are you going to show us that book?" Michael asked.

"The sumbook?" Ridge briefly touched his back pocket, as if to remind himself it was still there. "No. I told you, it's too dangerous."

"What is it, exactly? Will it burn out our eyeballs or something?"

"Burn out your eyeballs?"

"You said you couldn't open it because it was too dangerous."

Ridge was looking at him like he'd grown a second head, but if time travel was possible, who was to say there weren't books that could burn people's eyeballs? The logic made sense to Michael, though he now regretted the question because he realized it sounded babyish.

"It's dangerous because of what's written in it," Ridge said.

"Like, spells or something?" asked Michael.

"No. It's just summaries. That's why we call it a sumbook. My mom kind of invented them. No one really uses paper anymore, but she wanted something that could be taken to any timeprint. She has hundreds of them."

"A summary of what?" Gibby asked.

"Timeprints."

"What does that mean?" Michael asked.

"A timeprint is what we call a time period. When I left home, for example, the timeprint on the STM—the Spatial Teleportation Module—would have told my mom and my idiot brothers exactly what timeprint I traveled to. August seventeenth, 1999. When I left, we were studying Hurricane Floyd, which is in this sumbook, along with everything else that happened from 1980 to 2020. Well, not everything. There's no book big enough to fit *everything*. But the highlights. The sumbook is supposed to help STSs navigate the timeprint they—"

"What's an STS?" Gibby asked.

"Spatial teleportation scientist."

"Spatial teleportation scientist," Gibby repeated.

"Yeah. You know. Time traveler."

"Does that sumbook mention Y2K?" Michael asked. He thought of the toolbox in the kitchen. There were so many items in there that he hadn't thought to get. Screwdrivers. Hammers. Pliers.

"Please don't start with Y2K right now," Gibby said, rolling her eyes.

How could she roll her eyes? How could she not want to snatch the book away from Ridge? How could she not want to know?

"That book has information about the future, Gibby," said Michael. "The *future*. We could find out, right here and now, what will happen when the clocks turn over to January first. We could know exactly—"

"I don't want to discuss the sumbooks anymore," Ridge said. He pulled something out of his front pocket and cupped it in his hands. "I wanted someplace private to show you the device that brought me here, not to talk about sumbooks or anything that's going to happen in the future. I shouldn't have even mentioned it."

"You already told us something about the future, remember?" Michael said. "The earthquake?"

"Michael, please," Gibby said. She leveled her eyes at him. "I'm not even convinced he's telling us the truth. He could be completely insane."

"I'm not insane," Ridge said. "That's why I wanted to show you this."

Gibby leaned in.

Ridge opened his hands. He cradled the object inside like a delicate gem.

"What is it?" Gibby asked.

"It's what makes time travel possible."

Michael had never seen anything like it before. It was black and square—bigger than a postage stamp, smaller than a bar of soap. The device itself wasn't plastic, like a remote control, but it wasn't metal either. It slightly resembled a key fob. There was a small light on top, unlit.

It was familiar and unfamiliar all at once.

"It's called the EGG," Ridge said. "E-G-G."

"EGG," Gibby said. "What does that stand for?"

"It's the founder's initials."

"It doesn't look like much," Michael said. He fell back against the sofa. "You could've gotten it from the dumpster."

Ridge snorted. "Unlikely. This one EGG cost several trillion dollars."

"Wow," Gibby said. "What does it do?" She leaned farther in, her voice breathless with wonder, her hair brushing Ridge's wrists.

Michael stared at a dirty sock on the floor outside the bathroom door.

He didn't want to be here, in Beejee's apartment, with Gibby's hair brushing Ridge's arm, sitting this close to a book that had the information he needed.

"Okay," Ridge said. "Here's the situation. My mom is a scientist. She has a lab at UD on the Red Knot campus, and inside the lab is the STM. Spatial Teleportation Module. It's a prototype. A preliminary model for spatial teleportation . . . what you call time travel. The way it works is, you get inside the STM with this . . ." He nodded toward the EGG. "Then you input the Timestamp—the date you want to travel to—on an STM screen. You scan your thumbprint with the EGG, close your eyes, and *poof*, you're in 1999, or whatever date you put in. At the same coordinates as the STM."

"So if I scan my thumbprint on this thing, I'll travel into the future?" Gibby asked.

"No," Ridge said. "Only the person who activated the STM can use it again. My mom has fail-safes against everything." He paused. "Well, I guess not everything. Otherwise I wouldn't be here. But when I'm ready to go back, all I have to do is press my thumb against it and I'll rematerialize in the STM."

"What's that little light for?"

Ridge shrugged. "It's usually green. I guess it turns off while the STS is traveling. Since no one's done it before, it must—"

"Why did you want to come here on August seventeenth, 1999?" Michael asked.

What if it had something to do with his birthday? What if something terrible was just around the corner? Ridge had mentioned something about a hurricane . . . Hurricane Floyd. What if it had something to do with that?

"It was August seventeenth where I was, and I picked 1999 because it's my favorite year in history."

"1999 is your favorite year in history," Gibby repeated, deadpan. "Well, I guess I can see why. Look how glamorous this all is."

"I know it doesn't seem glamorous or interesting to you right now," Ridge said. "But that's because no one realizes they're living history every minute of every day. Sure, there are big moments, like the first Black president or the first trip to Mars and Jupiter, or the first STM. But the truth is, we're making history at this very moment, sitting on this couch together, looking at this EGG in these unfortunate living quarters. Every breath we take, we're contributing to history."

Michael split into two versions of himself: one who wanted to stay and hear what Ridge had to say, and another who wanted to go somewhere safe and familiar, where the answers to the future were out of reach instead of *literally* at his fingertips.

He wanted to stay so he wouldn't miss anything.

He wanted to leave so he would.

"I'm going to check on Mr. Mosley," he said, before he could change his mind. He shot off the couch like he was being launched from a cannon.

"But . . . ," Gibby said. "Don't you want to hear more?"

"No," said Michael. He walked into the kitchen and turned on the sink so he could wash Beejee's apartment from his hands. "If you want to stay, that's your business."

He was being childish, he knew. And maybe he shouldn't leave, just in case Ridge was criminally insane or something and Gibby needed Michael's protection.

Not that he would be able to do much protecting.

But he could check on Mr. Mosley.

That was one thing he could do.

The EGG, named for the Founder (See *Founder of Spatial Transportation*) is a handheld device that allows Spatial Teleportation Scientists (STSs) to teleport to and from a single date or timeprint through an immobile home base known as the Spatial Teleportation Module (STM).

The scientific mechanisms of the EGG are complex (See *EGG Scientific Mechanisms*), but the concept is relatively simple—by scanning an individual STS's thumbprint, the EGG dematerializes the STS into an individual energy pattern, which is subsequently rematerialized into the predestined timeprint, which is coded into the STM at the time of departure. Although current technology allows STSs to predetermine a timeprint, spatial scientists have not yet developed technology to select specific geographic landing destinations outside of the STM coordinates. Consequently, the STS will rematerialize in the exact location of the STM. Therefore, it is critical that STSs understand the landscape of their timeprint, so as not to rematerialize in a potentially dangerous situation, such as underwater, inside the foundation of a structure (such as concrete, brick walls, etc.), inside natural elements (rocks, trees, etc.), or within a large crowd.

Currently, the only existing STM is a prototype—known as STM1—located at latitude 39.605829 and longitude -75.718580, in the Spatial Teleportation Laboratory at the University of Delaware. Therefore, ST from STM1 would occur as follows:

1. STS enters the STM1 (39.605829, -75.718580) with EGG.

2. STS programs predestined TMP into the STM.

3. EGG scans thumbprint. STS engages in de- and rematerialization. (Please note that only the items in direct contact with the STS's person (i.e., in contact with the EGG) will engage in spatial transportation.)

4. STS rematerializes in predestined timeprint at 39.605829, -75.718580.

From Scientific Methods of Spatial Teleportation (ST)
Compiled by Maria Sabio, PhD, DST, Chief STS, University of Delaware

13

To Michael's surprise, Mosley was stretched across the couch, reading Gibby's book.

"I didn't think you were actually going to read it," Michael said as he returned the spare key to its hiding nook under the flowerpot.

Mosley's apartment didn't feel like home, exactly, but close enough. The one-bedroom layout was exactly like Beejee's, but it couldn't be more different. Everything about it was warm and comfortable, from the pillows on the sofa to the recliner where Michael now sat. Mosley's DVDs were shelved alphabetically in neat rows on his entertainment center. Sometimes Michael and his mom would stop by and borrow one. One of their favorites was *Raising Arizona*, with

Nicolas Cage, which Michael's mother let him watch even though it was PG-13.

"I didn't either, to tell you the truth," Mosley said, the book on his chest. A can of Dr Pepper sat on the end table. "But I figured, why not? I'm on page thirty and so far all I've learned is Melissa has a crush on Marc and Susan is the most popular girl in school. Someone better get murdered soon."

Michael laughed and looked around the apartment, hoping there was something he could do, some small task to keep himself busy and help Mr. Mosley at the same time. Instead, his eyes fell on the newspaper on the coffee table in front of him.

Quake Kills Thousands in Turkey. And the first paragraph: *Terrified earthquake survivors sought the safety of open ground Tuesday as the enormity of Turkey's tragedy became clear: more than 2,000 people killed, 10,000 injured, and thousands more missing.*

Two thousand people. Thousands more missing.

He picked up the newspaper, then returned it to the table, facedown.

"Do you need help with anything, Mr. Mosley? When I'm sick, all I want to do is lie around."

"Nah, I'm all right. My shoulder is giving me trouble from painting that darn apartment, that's all."

"I could help you paint next time."

"That's a nice offer, kiddo, but I'm pretty sure Ship would

fire me if I put one of the underage tenants to work."

"Well, that's what I'm good at—getting people fired," Michael said. The words leaped out of his mouth before he had time to turn them over. He was trying to be funny . . . at least that's what he told himself . . . but it didn't sound funny at all. He laughed.

Mosley dog-eared the book and sat up.

"You didn't get your mama fired. And she didn't get herself fired, either," he said. "It was one hundred percent Leonard Gibson. You understand?"

"Sure, I guess." Michael shrugged. "So do you need help with anything, or—"

"Listen," Mosley said. He put his elbows on his knees and leaned forward. "You didn't get your mama fired. You understand that, don't you?"

"I know what you're saying, Mr. Mosley, but the fact is, she wouldn't have been fired if I hadn't gotten the flu."

"Her son had the flu and she stayed home to take care of him, like the good mother she is. She never called out sick before that. Leonard Gibson had no business firing your mother."

"Why'd he do it, then?"

"Who knows why people do the things they do. Maybe he felt threatened because she's smarter than him. People with walnut-sized brains are afraid of smart people—especially smart *women*. Maybe he wanted to promote someone else, a buddy of his or something. Maybe he didn't like her because she didn't kiss his butt. Who knows why? It's not your job to figure out why walnut-brained people do walnut-brained things. It's your job to make sure you don't become one of those people." He pointed the book at Michael. "You know what my mama used to say? 'Before you go to sleep at night, ask yourself: was I the best person I could be today? If the answer is no, do better tomorrow.' I have a feeling Leonard Gibson has never asked himself that question a day in his life. But that's not your concern."

Michael paused. He heard what Mosley was saying, but the fact remained: no flu, no mom staying home, no getting fired. And now she was working three jobs.

"I had a cold last week and I did just fine at home by myself," Michael said. "I should have made her go to work."

"Ha!" Mosley said. "You can't make your mom do something she doesn't want to do. Besides, she's a grown woman, perfectly capable of making her own decisions. And just 'cause a person can take care of themselves all the time doesn't mean they should." He stretched out on the couch again. "You just focus on being eleven. That's hard enough."

"I'm twelve, remember?"

"Oh yes—how could I forget?" Mosley opened the book and unfolded the dog-ear. "That's even harder than eleven."

Especially when Y2K is just around the corner, Michael thought.

"So, do you need help with anything, Mr. Mosley?" he asked. "I could take out the trash or something."

"Nah, I'm okay, kiddo. I'm sure I'll be up and about soon." He turned to Michael. His eyes softened. "You know what? Maybe you could unload the dishwasher for me. I shouldn't pass up an offer of help. It's good to be taken care of sometimes. It's the way it ought to be."

"Sure!" Michael said.

Strange as it may sound, Michael enjoyed unloading the dishwasher at home. It didn't require much thought and it was a task with a clear beginning and end. No ambiguity.

The more dishes, the better.

Unfortunately, Mosley only had a few plates and a handful of silverware.

"It's not very full," Mosley admitted. "To be honest, sometimes I run it when I only have one plate and a fork. I like the sound. Makes me feel less alone. Pretty silly, huh?"

Michael stared at the four plates in front of him.

Who would take care of Mr. Mosley when Y2K hit?

We'll take him in, Michael thought. *He'll stay with us.*

Yes, it would be perfect. Why hadn't he thought of it before?

"No, it's not silly," Michael said. "Sometimes I talk to a water stain."

"I suppose we could do worse," Mr. Mosley said, chuckling. "People do strange things sometimes to remind themselves they're part of the world, don't they?"

"Yeah," Michael said. "They do."

AUDIO TRANSCRIPT

DATE
08/18/2199
LOCATION
UNIVERSITY OF DELAWARE DIGITAL LIBRARY
ARCHIVES
SECURE RESEARCH BOOTH 31498

SUBJECTS

SABIO, MARIA, ACTIVE LIBRARY PATRON (CARD#
02051997)
SABIO, SHALE, ACTIVE LIBRARY PATRON (CARD#
10131971)

HOLOLIBRARIAN:
Hello, Patron Maria Sabio. Hello, Patron
Shale Sabio. Welcome to the University of
Delaware Digital Library Archives. Please
state your request.

SABIO, MARIA:
Provide architectural archives on coordinates
39.605829, -75.718580 from January 1, 1990,
to December 31, 1999.

HOLOLIBRARIAN:
Your search will be complete in less than one
minute.

SABIO, MARIA:
Are you *sure* he went to the 1990s? He could
be anywhere.

SABIO, SHALE:
You know how obsessed he is with the 1990s.
Malls, music, all those terrible movies. If
he went anywhere, that's where he went.

HOLOLIBRARIAN:
From January 1, 1990, to December 31, 1999,
coordinates 39.605829, -75.718580 were as
follows. Intersection of Fox Run and Mink
Drive in unincorporated public neighborhood,
Red Knot, Delaware.

SABIO, MARIA:
An intersection. Oh god. What if he was hit
by a car? That used to happen to people.

HOLOLIBRARIAN:
Your request was not understood.

SABIO, SHALE:
It's an intersection in an unincorporated
public neighborhood, Mom. Which means there
probably weren't any cars around. And if
there were, they were probably moving really
slowly.

HOLOLIBRARIAN:
Your request was not understood.

SABIO, MARIA:
Provide statistics on how many people were
hit by cars in Red Knot, Delaware, from
January 1, 1990, to December 31, 1999.

HOLOLIBRARIAN:
Your search will be complete in less than
eight minutes.

SABIO, SHALE:
Cancel that request.

SHABIO, MARIA:
Shale!

HOLOLIBRARIAN:
Your search has been canceled.

SABIO, SHALE:
I don't think those statistics are going to
help, Mom. It won't tell us anything. We
should operate on the assumption that Ridge
arrived safely and wasn't hit by anything.
Right? That's how we'll get him back. We were
worried he rematerialized inside a tree or
something, and now we know it was probably
open air. So that's good. Right, Mom?

SABIO, MARIA:
Let's find out what was in the neighborhood.

SABIO, SHALE:
Provide architectural archival context for
immediate area surrounding coordinates
39.605829, -75.718580 from January 1, 1990,
to December 31, 1999.

HOLOLIBRARIAN:
Your search will be complete in less than one
minute.

SABIO, MARIA:
I can't believe this is happening. My son
could be anywhere. He could be *nowhere*. What
if he dematerialized and never—

HOLOLIBRARIAN:
From January 1, 1990, to December 31,
1999, contextual architecture surrounding
coordinates 39.605829, -75.718580 were as
follows. Public neighborhood. Unincorporated.
Fox Run apartment buildings. Nearby foliage
includes—

SABIO, MARIA:
Provide details on apartment buildings.

HOLOLIBRARIAN:
Details on apartment buildings near
coordinates 39.605829, -75.718580 are as
follows. Built 1987. Four hundred units.
Swimming pool. Basketball court. Office
building. Available parking with—

SABIO, MARIA:
Provide crime statistics of neighborhood from
January 1, 1990, to December 31, 1999.

HOLOLIBRARIAN:
Your search will be complete in less than
three minutes.

SABIO, SHALE:
Mom, I don't think—

HOLOLIBRARIAN:
Crime statistics for coordinates 39.605829,

-75.718580 from January 1, 1990, to December
31, 1999, are as follows. Approximately one
violent crime per one thousand residents.
Approximately ten property crimes per one
thousand residents.

SABIO, SHALE:
I don't think it's helpful for us to worry
about crime statistics, Mom.

HOLOLIBRARIAN:
Your request was not understood.

SABIO, SHALE:
Provide all available information on Ridge
Sabio from January 1, 1990, to December 31,
1999.

HOLOLIBRARIAN:
Your search will be complete in less than one
minute.

SABIO, SHALE:
If he left a mark, it should come up in the
archives, right?

SABIO, MARIA:
I don't know. I can't think straight.

HOLOLIBRARIAN:
No such records exist.

14

The apartment was quiet when Michael got home. He went straight to his room, turned on his new CD, and collapsed on the bed, Jordans and all. He thought of Mr. Mosley running the mostly empty dishwasher. He thought of the EGG and the sumbook. He thought of the people in Turkey, covered in dust and rubble. He thought of all the lights of the world flickering out, one by one. Water systems breaking down. Grocery stores looted. Highways clogged. Car accidents.

He thought of his mother.

He thought of what Ridge had said. *It's not one of those dangerous times.*

Michael didn't believe that. It was always a dangerous time. Danger lurked everywhere, especially when you weren't expecting it. Think of all those people in Turkey. Think of his mama, getting called into her boss's office and losing her job. Think of dads and moms who abandon their kids. Think of anything. It was all around. Waiting to strike. Just like Y2K.

"I'll take care of you, Mama," he whispered to the water stain. "And you too, Mr. Mosley."

He imagined himself showing them the stockpile under his bed.

I thought of everything—see?

I even remembered peaches.

At some point, Michael fell asleep. The telephone woke him up. It was still daylight outside—late afternoon. His head ached. Maybe he hadn't beaten that summer cold after all. He ambled to the kitchen and picked up the phone.

"Guess what," said Gibby, her voice happy on the other end of the line. "Beejee said Ridge could crash on his couch. He's even giving him some more stuff to wear and letting him take a shower. I had to promise part of my paycheck, but whatever."

"You think this guy is an actual *time traveler*?" Michael said. "So you believe him?"

"Well, we spent the afternoon hanging out and . . . yeah . . . I do. Do you?"

Michael didn't answer.

"Maybe you should have stayed," Gibby said. "Also, it wasn't cool to leave like that. What if he was a serial killer, like you said yesterday?"

"I don't know," Michael finally said. "Sorry."

"Look," Gibby said. "Tomorrow is a babysitting day—well, *half* a babysitting day, since I have to go to work in the afternoon—and I'm taking him to the mall. That means you have to come with. Okay?" She paused. "It's funny, don't you think? Of all the things he wants to see before he leaves. The *mall.*"

"Yeah," Michael said, unsmiling. "Funny."

1. Do not reveal information about things to come, especially if Native Timeprint Inhabitants (NTIs) have a reasonable ability to manipulate said events. In cases where NTIs do not have a reasonable ability to manipulate events, it is still best to withhold information.

2. STSs should always err toward observation.

   2.1. Do not interact with NTIs unless absolutely necessary.

   2.2. Do not engage in social activities in which you may interact with NTIs.

   2.3. Do not visit social settings that may involve large groups of NTIs.

From Best Practices for Responsible Spatial Teleportation (ST)
Compiled by Maria Sabio, PhD, DST, Chief STS, University of Delaware

15

When Ridge stepped out of Beejee's apartment at 9:45, he was wearing old cargo pants—Michael could see the outline of the sumbook resting inside the buttoned front pocket— and a Hootie and the Blowfish T-shirt. Michael was wearing his Jordans, a clean pair of jeans, and one of the few T-shirts he owned that didn't have a hole in it.

"How are we getting there?" Ridge asked. "The bus? The train? Uber?"

"We're taking Eloise," Gibby proclaimed. She had on a yellow sundress that Michael had never seen before. And it looked like she was wearing makeup. Her eyes were more sparkly than usual.

"Ooo! What's an Eloise?" Ridge was bouncy and

smiley, like a kid going to an amusement park.

"You'll see," Gibby said.

Michael didn't have to ask. He already knew Eloise—aka Gibby's 1987 red Toyota Corolla that had a cassette tape jammed in the player.

Michael lingered behind as they walked toward the parking lot. Tuxedo darted in front of them and slipped behind one of the bushes. Michael wished he could follow. He didn't feel like going to the mall. He didn't like the mall. And he'd been so anxious and uneasy the night before that he'd hardly slept.

All those people. All those friend groups. All those kids getting back-to-school clothes. The only potential upside to the Y2K disaster was the fact that it might disrupt the school year. Every time the idea of seventh grade popped into Michael's head, he pushed it way, way down and thought of other things instead.

"There she is! Eloise!" Gibby said, pointing to the Toyota with her keys. "My car."

Ridge jogged ahead, his mouth in a perfect circle.

"I can't believe I'm going to ride in an actual *car* from the twentieth century!" he said, peeking through Eloise's windows. He climbed into the driver's seat as soon as Gibby opened the door. He put his hands on the steering wheel and pretended to drive.

"Wow," he said. He beeped the horn once. "Wow!" He beeped it again, louder.

"Okay, Dale Earnhardt, get in the passenger seat," Gibby said, waving him over.

Michael slid into the back seat and buckled up without a word. Eloise smelled like old, dirty plastic. Usually he loved Eloise. But today she was a traitor.

Ridge knocked the car out of gear and banged against the glove compartment as he moved over to the other seat, saying, "Dale Earnhardt, American race-car driver, born April twenty-ninth, 1951. Died February eighteenth—" He clamped his mouth shut. "Never mind."

"How do you know about Dale Earnhardt?" Gibby asked.

"I read about him in my pop culture omnibus, and I have an eidetic memory," Ridge said. He pulled at the seat belt, trying to figure out how it worked.

"What's an eidetic memory?" Michael muttered. He didn't feel like making conversation, but sometimes curiosity got the best of him.

But Ridge wasn't listening. He was operating the seat belt like it was a complicated feat of modern engineering. Gibby finally secured it for him, laughing, which made Michael sink farther into his seat. When she put the key in the ignition, Ridge watched like it was the most wondrous thing he'd ever experienced. When Eloise roared to life, he jumped, startled, then craned his neck this way and that, studying every inch of the Corolla.

"This is amazing," he said.

"Not as amazing as the music," said Gibby. She winked at Michael, which did nothing to lift his spirits.

Okay, maybe it did a *little* to lift his spirits.

Gibby turned up the volume and an all-too-familiar song came to life. "Cracklin' Rosie" by Neil Diamond. It blasted from the cassette that'd been stuck in Eloise's tape player for years. It had been there when Gibby bought Eloise, and she refused to dislodge it. "Eloise loves Neil Diamond," she had explained to Michael the first time she'd given him a ride.

Back then, Michael thought that Neil Diamond was terrible and he suspected Gibby did too, but after a few trips, the music morphed into something else—an inside joke. And now Ridge was in on it too.

Ridge scrunched up his nose. "What is this?"

"Neil Diamond!" Gibby said, smiling at Michael in the rearview mirror as she put Eloise in reverse.

"I've listened to an embarrassing amount of pop music from the 1990s, but I don't ever recall encountering this," Ridge said.

"That's because Neil is *adult contemporary*," Gibby said. "And he is an acquired taste."

"Adult contemporary," Ridge repeated. "Sounds awful."

Michael rested his head against the window as they pulled out of the apartment complex. Usually riding in Gibby's car made him feel older. Important. *I have places to go. See me in this car?* But today he felt like an interloper.

It was a twenty-minute drive to Christiana Mall. Ridge spent the entire journey looking out the window, mouth half open. Everything fascinated him—street signs, traffic, traffic lights, speed bumps, speed limits, medians, fast-food restaurants, police cars, fire trucks.

Gibby laughed at many of his questions, then turned the volume down and said, "Tell us what it's like where you're from. Are there flying cars and hoverboards and stuff?"

Ridge paused. "Everything is different. It's like another planet."

"What do people do for fun?" asked Gibby.

"I spend my days at the academy. Studying."

"Is that what everyone does in the future? Study?"

Ridge paused. "No. That's just what my family does. We're scientists. Supposedly we're going to be the world's first spatial teleportation scientists."

"Not supposedly," Gibby said. "You did it. Right?"

"Yeah," Ridge said, his face serious. "And after this, the whole program will probably get shut down. Who knows what's going on back home?" He frowned. "I don't even want to think about it."

When the exit for Mall Road came into view, Michael leaned forward and said, "Did the world change a lot after Y2K? People think society will have to restart after January first, just like the computers. Some say we'll have to learn how to rely on instincts rather than artificial intelligence, and pretty soon, all the technology—like the internet and chat rooms and stuff—will disappear."

"Y2K was a really long time ago," Ridge said.

"It hasn't even happened yet," Michael said.

"Trust me, you're better off not worrying about the future. Focus on the here and now. That's what I'm doing," Ridge said. He was still looking out the window. He hadn't stopped. "The first state of being."

"The first state of what?" Gibby said.

"The first state of being," he said. "That's what my mom calls the present moment. It's the first state of existence. It's right now, this moment, in this car. The past is the past. The future is the future. But this, right now? This is the first state, the most important one, the one in which everything matters. That's why I'm not going to think about the mess I left behind. That's the third state—the future. I'll worry about that when I get there. For now, I want to be here and now, listening to this terrible music with the two of you."

Christiana Mall appeared ahead.

"It's not terrible, it's an *acquired taste*," Gibby said. She turned up the volume as they turned into the parking lot. Neil was singing "Kentucky Woman" now. Gibby sang along—off-key, of course. When the song was over, she said, "There's a lot of rhinestones in this world, Ridge, but there's only one Diamond!"

As far as Michael was concerned, they couldn't find a parking space fast enough.

16

Ridge didn't say so, but it was obvious that malls did not exist in his future. And if they did, they were nothing like the Christiana Mall in Newark, Delaware. As soon as he stepped through the entrance, he froze, mouth agape. He turned to his left. He turned to his right. He looked at the ceiling. He looked at the floor. He studied the mall map like it was the Declaration of Independence.

"So this is a mall," he said, peering at the list of stores. "'A popular meeting place for American teenagers.'"

"Is that from your sumbook?" Michael asked.

"For the record, I'm an American teenager and I hate the mall," said Gibby.

"Why would you hate the mall?" Ridge asked.

"It opened ten minutes ago and look at all the people here already," she said. "Too crowded. And I always see people from school."

Michael was already scanning the environment for former classmates.

"Why wouldn't you want to see people from school?" Ridge asked.

Gibby shrugged. "I don't mind seeing them *at* school. But if I wanted to see them *away* from school, I'd make plans with them. Plans that do not involve the mall."

Ridge moved forward like a man on a mission. "I think it's remarkable," he said.

Ridge explored every single store—Lord & Taylor, Williams-Sonoma, even the Watch Station—as Gibby walked beside him and Michael lagged silently behind.

"Isn't it dangerous for you to be here?" Michael finally said, after ten minutes inside Pottery Barn, of all places. "You could be destroying the what-do-you-call-it. The continuum."

Ridge tugged at the pull string of a display lamp. "You sound like my mother," he said. "But according to the Saeed Theory, if I was destroying the continuum, it would have already been destroyed in 2199, and I would not have been able to come here in the first place, because I would cease to exist."

"Well, whatever," Michael muttered, barely understanding

a word Ridge had said. "It seems really irresponsible for you to be at the mall."

When the three of them walked out of Pottery Barn, Michael continued, "I mean it. We've already got Y2K to worry about, and now this."

"Michael," Gibby said, stopping in front of the Piercing Pagoda. "Enough about Y2K."

"What's a Piercing Pagoda?" Ridge asked.

A girl sat on the piercing stool while an employee steadied the gun. Before either Michael or Gibby could answer Ridge's question, the piercing gun went off, sending a stud through the girl's earlobe. She wailed at the top of her lungs.

Ridge gasped. "What the—"

Gibby pulled on Ridge's sleeve to move him along. "She's just getting her ears pierced. Don't people have pierced ears where you're from?"

Ridge rubbed his own earlobes as they walked away. "Kind of. But not exactly."

"Whatever," Michael said. KB Toys was ahead; he slow-jogged toward it. Normally he would try to act cool, like he was too old for toys and didn't care about KB, but if no one was going to listen to him and Gibby was going to giggle with Ridge and sing Neil Diamond, then what was the point? Besides, there was a display table out front with an ENTER TO WIN sign. Unfortunately, it was for a LEGO MindStorms

Robotics Discovery Set, and Michael had zero interest in LEGO or robotics. He stopped anyway. He was too annoyed. The seed of resentment in his stomach had cracked open, sprouted bitter branches.

Gibby came up next to him. "Why are you being so snappy all of a sudden?" she whispered. She picked up the pad of entry slips and tapped it absently on the display table.

Michael pretended to be intensely interested in the fishbowl full of entries.

"I'm not," he said. He glanced at Ridge, who was inspecting a game of Clue. "I'm just saying, if he's really from the future—which I guess he is—then everything he's doing could be bad. Like, really bad. Remember in *Back to the Future* when Marty almost disintegrates?"

"This isn't a movie, Michael," Gibby said. Babysitter voice. "And what if you're wrong? What if nothing bad happens? What if something *good* happens? You always think of the bad things."

Michael wanted to say something snarky, but he didn't. It would only prove her point.

Besides, he thought of good things sometimes—didn't he?

Gibby placed the pad in front of him. "You should fill one out. Enter to win this robotics thing. You never know. Maybe something good will happen." She reached around the fishbowl for the pen, clicked it open, and gave it to him. "You need a hobby, anyway."

He stared at the paper and pen.

You need a hobby, anyway.

What was that supposed to mean?

Even if he did "need a hobby," it wouldn't be this. He didn't like stupid LEGOs or stupid robotics or stupid anything. If she knew anything about him, she would know that.

He picked up the pen and filled out her information instead.

"Maybe *you* need a hobby," he muttered.

17

After KB Toys, Michael announced he was going to Waldenbooks. If Gibby thought he needed a hobby, he'd show her one—he'd go find one of those Christopher Pike books she had on her desk and buy one of his own with the twenty bucks Mr. Mosley had given him. Then she'd see he was smart *and* he wasn't the little kid she thought he was.

Ridge had been enchanted by all the toys at KB, but his eyes shined when he heard about the bookstore. He quickly put away the Bowser action figure he'd been inspecting and followed Michael. So did Gibby. For once, Michael was in the lead.

"What is Bowser?" Ridge asked.

"What?" Michael said, distracted.

"That toy was named Bowser. From something called Mario Kart. What is a Mario Kart?"

Michael kept walking. How do you explain Mario Kart to someone?

"Don't they have video games in the future?" Michael asked.

"Yes. Well. Sort of." Ridge paused. "Hey, what's that box over there?"

He was pointing to a photo booth now.

"We should get our pictures taken!" Gibby suggested.

Michael picked up his pace. He didn't want to know who she meant by "we."

"Probably not a good idea," said Ridge. "What with the time traveling and all."

Ridge was at Michael's heels when they arrived at Waldenbooks. Michael made a beeline for the fiction section, but Ridge slowed down.

"I can't believe this," he said. "How incredible." He opened his arms wide. "A bookstore!"

"Shh," Gibby whispered. The guy behind the counter—COLBY, his name tag said—raised his eyebrows at them.

Michael found two Christopher Pike books on a shelf near the back. *Gimme a Kiss* and *Remember Me*. Neither of those sounded remotely interesting to Michael, but *Remember Me* was about a ghost, which sounded more promising than some book with "kiss" in the title, so he picked it up, even though he didn't even like reading that much.

The only book he'd ever really liked was *The Giver*, by Lois Lowry. He was supposed to give a report on it in front of the class last year. He had memorized his entire presentation and practiced over and over at the bathroom mirror, but when the day came, he forgot everything he meant to say and stood there, in front of everyone, in a stupor. His classmates blinked back at him, giggling, until he finally blurted out, "I need to go to the bathroom," and then their giggles turned into all-out laughter.

Anyway. No need to think about that now. That was eleven-year-old Michael. Twelve-year-old Michael was buying a book of his own. *Remember Me*, by Christopher Pike.

But—

If he *really* wanted to impress Gibby, maybe he should buy a book that was thicker than Christopher Pike. More complicated. A serious, grown-up book.

He slipped *Remember Me* back in place and moved to another shelf, where he found a nice-looking, thick, dense book called *Our Angry Earth*, by Isaac Asimov and Frederik Pohl. The cover appeared very, very serious—big white letters against a black background with a single red sun smack in the middle. All of Gibby's books had illustrations of the characters, but this had nothing of the sort. Just the title, the authors, and a quote from Michael McCloskey of the Sierra Club, whatever that meant.

"The one ecology book to read," McCloskey said.

No doubt about it. This was just the kind of boring book a smart, mature person would read.

He walked toward the magazines holding *Our Angry Earth* face-out so Gibby could see it, but she wasn't there anymore. Ridge was by himself with an issue of *National Geographic* pressed against his face. He was taking big, deep breaths while Colby eyed him curiously from the counter.

"Look at this, Michael," Ridge said. "Look at this magazine. It smells amazing. And the paper! I've never felt paper like this before. Touch it. You won't believe it."

Michael obligingly touched the paper while keeping an eye on Colby.

"Maybe keep your voice down a little," Michael said. "That guy is looking at you like you're from another planet."

But Ridge was barely listening. He turned the pages slowly and delicately, like he was handling a precious ancient artifact.

He paused at a photo of a Siberian tiger. "Look at this, Michael," he said. "Isn't it beautiful?"

Michael looked at the photo, wondering where Gibby was. He'd never heard a guy—much less a *teenage* guy—use the word "beautiful."

"This photo was taken recently," Ridge said.

It *was* a beautiful picture, Michael had to admit. The tiger was lying down, staring directly at the lens, with the sun setting behind him. The tiger looked fierce, strong, confident, like nothing could ever harm it.

"There are tigers on Earth right now," Ridge said, more to himself than anyone. He turned the pages, inhaling with each turn. He held the magazine up so Michael could sniff too.

"Smell," Ridge said.

"No, thanks."

"No, really. Smell it."

"I don't need to."

Ridge lifted the magazine to Michael's nose. "Yes, you do. You really do."

"Okay, okay," Michael said. He took a big whiff. "You're right. That *does* smell pretty good."

"Umm . . . *what* are you two doing?"

Gibby. Her head was tilted in mock amusement. When had she sauntered up? And she wasn't alone, either. Two girls stood with her. One was a redhead, about Gibby's age. The other was a younger girl wearing a Phillies cap.

"Uh," Michael said.

"Look what I found." Ridge showed them the magazine. "It's remarkable, isn't it?"

The redhead raised her eyebrows.

"This is Ridge," Gibby said quickly. She motioned toward the redhead. "And this is Teresa. We go to Red Knot together. Told you I always see people from school. Teresa's in the theater club. We had algebra together."

Teresa stuck out her tongue. "Yuck. I hated that class."

Gibby shrugged. "It wasn't so bad."

"Of course it wasn't bad for you, Miss Straight As," Teresa said good-naturedly, as she put her hand on top of the younger girl's head. "This is my little sister, Paige."

Paige smiled. She had a big, bright smile that lit up her whole face. She pointed at Michael's shirt. "I like them too." She leaned forward and whispered, "They're way better than Hootie and the Blowfish."

Michael suddenly forgot how to speak. His brain tried to calculate what she was saying.

"This is Michael," Ridge said, nudging him.

"Oh," said Michael. "Yeah. I'm Michael." He looked away from Paige and realized Ridge was wearing Beejee's Hootie T-shirt. And he was wearing a Red Hot Chili Peppers T-shirt.

"Do you go to Red Knot Middle?" Paige asked. "I'm going into seventh."

"So is Michael," Gibby offered, smiling.

"I don't recognize you," Paige said. "Did you go there last year?"

"No," Michael said. He wanted to say more, but what?

"Oh, so you're new to the school," Paige said. Somehow her smile grew even bigger and brighter. "I can show you around."

Teresa rolled her eyes. "Paige is like a one-woman welcoming committee. She's on the student council." She looked at Gibby and Ridge. "They do all that goody-goody stuff."

"You mean, like being *nice* and *doing good deeds?*" Paige said.

"Excuse me," Teresa said, hands on hips. "I do good deeds all the time. Who took you to the emergency room yesterday when you got stung?"

"It was urgent care, not the ER," Paige said. "And only because Mom made you."

Teresa shrugged. "Still. I drove."

"Wait—" Ridge said. He looked directly at Paige. "What stung you?"

"A bee!" Paige said proudly. "Wanna see?" Before anyone could answer, she pulled up her sleeve and showed them a faint pink welt with a bright red dot in the center. "It was a lot worse yesterday."

Ridge touched her arm delicately with the tips of two fingers.

"Wow," he said.

His eyes sparkled. Glistened. Like he was about to *cry*.

Michael glanced toward Colby to see if he was watching them from the counter, but he wasn't.

Gibby pushed Ridge's hands out of the way and said, "We better get going. Don't you think, guys?" She looked at Ridge, then Michael, then Ridge again. Her eyes were wide, like "Stop acting so weird."

Teresa bumped Paige with her hip. "You should give Michael your phone number before they leave, in case you want to meet up on the first day."

Michael's face burned with embarrassment. He hoped no one noticed. He'd never been given a girl's number before, except Gibby's, but that didn't really count.

"Good idea!" said Paige. She reached into her pocket, pulled out a gum wrapper, then darted off to the counter to get a pen.

Teresa smiled at Michael. "Paige knows everyone at Red Knot Middle."

When Paige came back, she handed Michael the crumpled paper with her name and phone number written on it. Paige Kaminski. The dots on the Is were hearts.

He didn't know what to say.

Then he thought of his mama.

All you have to do is say thank you.

"Thank you," he said.

Threats to the bee population became a global concern starting in 2006, when beekeepers first reported significant colony losses. The failure of bee colonies was caused by a wide range of factors, including but not limited to pathogens, pests, pesticides, pollutants, habitat loss, climate variability, agricultural production intensification, and crop management practices.

Although colony losses occurred steadily through 2020, there were several years in which beekeepers reported sustainable colonies and it looked as though bees might have escaped danger. Unfortunately, the colony losses from 2006 to 2020 were a precursor to a much larger crisis to come, which ultimately resulted in the Global Famine of 2100. Genetically engineered bees were developed in 2092, but could only provide sixty-three percent of natural function.

In the modern world, fewer than 100 managed bee colonies remain. The wild bee population is now extinct. The last wild bee was observed in June 2100. (See *Summary Book 2120–2150*.)

Excerpt from The Spatial Teleportation Summary Book for the Turn of the Twenty-First Century (1980–2020), *compiled by Maria Sabio, PhD, DST, Chief STS, University of Delaware, translated from Original Eaker Linton Code*

18

Gibby drove them back to Fox Run after a few hours because she had to go to work. She considered calling in sick so they could do something fun, like go to the movies, but Michael talked her out of it. "Remember what happened to my mom," he said. *She called out sick and got fired.*

He didn't need to remind her who had fired her.

In Michael's apartment, the Rosarios' answering machine blinked with a single message.

Ridge, enamored by the "antiquated technology," asked if he could press the button.

"Sure, go ahead," Michael said as he set his Waldenbooks bag on the counter. He and Ridge both had milkshakes from Johnny Rockets, compliments of Gibby. The milkshake had dulled what was left of Michael's irritability.

He'd almost forgotten about the sumbook in Ridge's pocket.

Almost.

Mr. Mosley's voice came from the answering machine.

"Hey, Michael," Mosley said. "I stopped by for lunch, but you weren't home. I'll be around tomorrow. Hope you're off doing something fun."

Michael glanced at the clock. It was just after one thirty.

Ridge set down his milkshake, picked up the phone, and studied it from every angle, his face bright with curiosity. "Can we call someone? Can we *please* call someone?"

"We can call Mr. Mosley back, if you want."

Michael motioned for the phone, but Ridge brought it to his chest.

"Can I dial the numbers?" he asked.

"Sure." Michael gave him the number. Ridge dutifully pushed each one on the keypad and listened intently as Mr. Mosley's phone rang.

"It's ringing!" Ridge said excitedly.

"That's typically what happens." Michael motioned for the phone. When Mr. Mosley answered, he said, "Hey, Mr. Mosley. Sorry I wasn't here for lunch. We went to the mall."

"Get anything good?"

"I bought a book."

"Does anyone get murdered in it?"

"Not that I know of. Are you feeling better?"

"A little bit, I suppose. Sometimes all you need is a good rest," Mr. Mosley said. "I'll be around tomorrow with some sandwiches, all right?"

"All right," Michael said.

As soon as Michael returned the phone to its cradle, Ridge said, "I always wondered what it was like to talk on a twentieth-century phone."

"How do phones work where you're from?"

Ridge hesitated. "I'm not sure how to explain. It's complicated."

They relocated to the couch with their milkshakes. Michael turned on the television. *The Ricki Lake Show* filled the screen.

"Some people say that there will be a twelve-month disruption of daily life when Y2K hits," Michael said casually. "No electrical power, no clean water, no telecommunications. Food, gas, and retail shortages. The stock market will crash. No one will have jobs. There will be riots."

Ridge took a sip of his milkshake. He shook the cup around. "Is this Styrofoam?"

"Yes."

"Styrofoam doesn't exist anymore. Neither does plastic."

Michael stared absently at Ricki Lake as she interviewed

a couple about the boyfriend's roving eye. "How come you can tell us about plastic and Styrofoam and earthquakes, but you can't tell me about Y2K?"

"Because there's nothing you can really do about any of those things. You're just one kid."

"Well, if I'm just one kid, then I can't do anything about Y2K either."

"That's not true. There's plenty of things you could do. Let's say I tell you, 'Michael, everything you're worried about is going to happen, just like you said.' You could panic and tell everyone in this apartment complex, which could start an organized survivalist effort, which could result in the riots you just told me about. Or you could ransack a grocery store for supplies and a shelf could fall on you and send you to the hospital. Then again, if I say, 'Michael, nothing is going to happen. No disaster will come to pass,' then you could tell all your friends that they don't need to worry, and you could go on the news and tell everyone it's all a big buildup to nothing. No one worries, everyone stops preparing, and a disaster happens as a result."

"But I'm just one kid. No one will listen to me. Plus I don't have any friends," Michael said.

"What about those kids with the basketball?"

"I thought you said there was some theory, the Saeed Theory or whatever, which meant that nothing you do here will change anything, so it was okay to tell us stuff."

"It's a lot more complicated than that," Ridge said. "Are they friends of yours?"

"Who?"

"The kids with the basketball."

"The Prince brothers? No."

"Why not?"

"Because they're just not, okay? Let's go back to talking about Y2K. You once said something about the continuum, and how whatever's happening now has already happened. Right?"

"Word," Ridge said.

"So if you tell me about Y2K, it'll be fine. Because if it *wasn't* fine, your timeline would be all screwed up. Right?"

Ridge sneezed.

"Is that a yes?" Michael said.

"No. Because there's also the possibility that I never tell you about Y2K, which is precisely why my timeline is intact," Ridge said. He wiped his nose on his sleeve and took a swig of his milkshake. "You might as well drop the subject, Michael. I'm never going to tell you what happens. Not when it's only a few months away. It would be phenomenally stupid of me."

"Yes, but—"

"So, what's the problem with the Princes? What, are they jerks or something?"

"Wait. What?"

"The brothers."

"That's not what we're talking about."

"It is now."

Michael sighed and stared at the television. A commercial for the new iMac was playing. Jeff Goldblum. "Seems like everybody these days is on the internet, right?" he was saying.

"They're friendly," said Michael. "But . . ."

"But what?"

"Well. They're brothers."

"So?"

So, they're a unit all by themselves. What use do they have for me?

The scenarios clicked through his head. Him, missing every basket by a mile. Him, tripping on his own shoelaces. Him, getting body-checked and crashing to the concrete. Them: "Why did we invite this kid?"

"You have a weighted mind," Ridge said. "That's what my mom calls it when people carry a lot of worries and anxieties—a weighted mind. Because it can feel heavy. Some people get upgrades for it where I'm from."

"What do you mean, upgrades?"

"You can get artificial upgrades for certain things. My mom says it's not really an upgrade, though, because upgrade implies that all our so-called imperfections are problematic, and she says that's not true. The Global Science Council agrees. But the AI companies—the ones who offer the upgrades—think the GSC is wrong. They say it's another era of human evolution. There's a lot of debate on the topic." He set down his milkshake and pinched the bridge of his nose, like he was getting a headache just thinking about it. "My mom loves debate, though. She even named me after one."

"I don't think I'd want to get an upgrade, or whatever you call it," Michael said. He imagined sitting in a booth, getting injected with microchips. Some people said that's where the internet would lead—straight into a digital age where everyone would be scanned like groceries. "Does it hurt? Have you done it?"

"No."

Michael imagined having all his imperfections corrected. No more awkwardness. No more freezing in front of the class. Always knowing just what to say and when to say it.

Maybe an upgrade wouldn't be so bad after all.

"Do people get sick in the future?"

"Not very often. There are some things that are unavoidable, but we have this thing called the HUCK. You put a patch on, and you're better within minutes." Ridge shrugged, like it was no big deal.

"What does HUCK stand for?"

"Health Ukash-Chekole Kit."

"What is 'Ukash-Chekole'?"

"It's named after the two women who invented it."

Michael had more questions—*What does it feel like when you put the patch on? How do people die if they never get sick? Are there patches for other things too? If I lived in the future, could I get an upgrade to make myself as big as Beejee?*—but a commercial for Super Smash Mario Brothers came on and diverted Ridge's attention.

"Hey, it's a show about that toy!" he said, pointing at the television. "Bowser!"

"It's not a show. It's a commercial," Michael said.

"Do you have one of those Nintendo 64s?"

"No. We can't afford it."

"Oh. Too bad."

Ricki Lake came back on.

"What do you mean, your mom named you after a debate?" Michael asked.

Ridge set his milkshake aside. "There's this stupid document in the founder's hall of the GSC museum, and it has one word written on it. *Ridge.* It's encased under glass and everything. All they know is that the paper belonged to the founder, but they have no idea what it means. Scientists have been arguing about it for centuries. Some people think it refers to the dunes on the Delaware coast. Some people think it has something to do with brain function. Others think it doesn't mean anything. My mom says she has no idea, she just likes the mystery. All I know is, it's really annoying being named after a piece of paper, especially when you're surrounded by scientists all the time."

"I was named after my father, except he goes by Mike. That's why . . . hey, are you all right?"

Ridge was pressing on his throat with his fingers.

"I think this milkshake is irritating my throat," he said.

"Maybe it's too cold," Michael said.

"Yeah," Ridge said. "Maybe."

Then he sneezed again.

The **Ridge Document Mystery** refers to a single slip of paper discovered among the founder's personal documents. (See *Founder*.) The paper would have been disregarded as meaningless had it not been encased in a glass frame, hinting at greater importance. The opposite side of the document once had verbiage, but the image has faded with age and is impossible to decipher, despite numerous attempts by modern science.

The scientific community has never been able to attach any significance or meaning to the word "ridge." There are various theories, all of which have sparked spirited debate. Some believe "ridge" may refer to ancient sand dunes, which are common morphologic features along the Delmarva Peninsula, which is 170 miles long and includes the vast majority of Delaware and parts of the Eastern Shore regions of Maryland and Virginia. Others believe it could refer to gyri, the ridges on the outer surface of the brain. Still others believe it could relate to an unknown architectural structure.

From *The Encyclopedia Britannica-Barlowe* *(2199)*

19

Of all the items in the Rosario household, nothing fascinated Ridge more than the microwave. Michael heated Hot Pockets for dinner, and Ridge watched the plate turn. When the Hot Pockets were done—ham and cheese, Michael's favorite—Ridge was barely interested in eating.

"Beejee doesn't have one of these in his apartment," Ridge said, tapping the glass. "How does it work? The sumbook doesn't mention microwaves."

"I don't know how it works. It just . . . works." Michael shrugged.

"Let's microwave more things," Ridge said. He opened a cabinet over the microwave—the one Michael could never quite reach—and snatched a bag of gummy bears. "What about this?"

"Those belong to my mom. They're her favorites," Michael said. He made a mental note to add gummy bears to the stockpile. "Besides, you can't put gummy bears in the microwave."

"Why?"

"I don't know. You just don't. They'd probably explode."

Ridge tossed the gummy bears aside and picked up a packet of Kool-Aid. "What about this?"

"Let's not put anything else in the microwave. I don't want to waste food. Let's just eat what we have." Michael motioned toward the cooling Hot Pockets on the counter, then looked around as if seeing his home for the first time. He'd never had anyone over before, besides Gibby; it was strange to see it through someone else's eyes. "Sorry we don't have a table. Our apartment's kinda small. We can eat on the couch, if you want, or you can sit on Mr. Mosley's stool."

But Ridge wasn't paying attention. He lifted and examined the Hot Pocket. "What's in this?"

"Ham and cheese." Michael took a big bite of his. He was famished.

Ridge bit a small corner and chewed thoughtfully.

"This is delicious," he said, taking another bite.

"I know," Michael replied. Mouth full, he said, "How do you reheat food in the future?"

Ridge licked a drip of cheese from the side of his mouth. "It's complicated."

"That's what you said about the phones."

"I know." Ridge shrugged. "But some things are hard to explain because two or three inventions have to happen before my explanation would make any sense. It would be like explaining the internet to someone who doesn't know what electricity is."

"How about yes or no questions?"

"Hmm. Maybe. As long as they're big-picture questions. And nothing about the immediate future. No Y2K."

"Okay." Now that Michael had the opportunity to rattle off questions, his mind went blank. Strangely enough, his first thought was Tuxedo and Clipper. "Are there cats in the future? Little cats, like the one who sat with you on the bench."

"Yes."

"What about dogs?"

"Definitely."

"Allergies?"

"No."

"Schools?"

"Unfortunately."

"Cars?"

"Not like Eloise."

"Flying cars?"

"Complicated."

"Cancer?"

"Yes. But no one dies from it anymore, because of the HUCK."

"Robots?"

"Yes, but we don't call them that."

"What do you call them?"

"Confidential." Ridge licked the last of the cheese from his fingers.

"Jet packs?"

"What's a jet pack?"

"Like, a backpack that you put on and then fly off somewhere."

"No."

Michael rinsed their plates and slipped them into the dishwasher. Then he walked into the living room and said, "Television? Movies?"

"Yes and yes." Ridge fell back onto the sofa.

"Crime?"

"Yes."

Michael glanced at his sneakers by the door. "Jordans?"

Ridge laughed. "No."

"Basketball?"

"Yes. But it's a little different."

"How long do people live?"

"That's not a yes or no question. But they live a lot longer than people do today."

Michael bit the inside of his cheek, thinking. "Are people happy in the future?"

"I guess it depends on who you ask."

"What do people do for fun?"

"Depends on who they are." Ridge paused. A mischievous look crossed his face. "But sometimes—most definitely— people contact other people when they get their numbers."

"What does that mean?"

"Well. You know how people call each other on the phone here? Everyone has their own number and everything?"

"Yeah."

"It's similar in the future too. I mean, obviously our technology is better. But the concept is still the same. When I have a girl's number, I make sure to use it. How else am I supposed to get to know her?"

Michael narrowed his eyes. "What are you trying to say?"

"I'm just *saying*. For example, there's this girl back home, Aderlaine. I asked her if she wanted to go stargazing with me a few days ago because she's really into astronomy and all that. I knew there was a chance she'd say no, but I figured, I have two options. One, I never ask her, and I'm *guaranteed* not to take her stargazing. Or two, I ask, and then I *might* go stargazing. Option two is definitely the smarter option, don't you think?"

Before Michael could answer, Ridge continued, "There's this philosopher named Mel Conklin. My mom is always quoting her. She says the Conklin Principle goes like this: For every bad outcome you can anticipate, you should consider *at least* one positive outcome. Scientists have to anticipate everything that can go wrong with their research and experiments—it's part of what a good scientist does. But a *great* scientist never forgets the Conklin Principle, according to my mom."

"So you took the girl stargazing?"

"That's not the point," Ridge said. "And anyway, we're talking about you."

"Me?"

"Yeah. I think you should call that girl. Paige."

"No way."

"Way."

"Why?"

"Why? For the reasons I just said. To get to know her, to ask her if she wants to go do something, like go to the mall."

"I don't even know if I like her," Michael said, but even as the words drifted out of his mouth, he thought about her smile and how it lit up her whole face. "What if I call and it's awkward and no one knows what to say? I mean, I don't even know her."

"That's third-state thinking. You'll never get anywhere if you what-if everything. You've got to live in the now. The first state."

"The first state," Michael repeated.

Ridge nodded. "Right here, right now. It's the best place to be."

20

Michael heard the front door open at ten thirty, long after Ridge had gone back to Beejee's.

Michael was already in bed. The sidewalk lights cast a subtle light in the darkness. "Mom, is that you?" he called. It was a silly question—of course it was her.

She opened his door and poked her head inside. She hadn't put her purse down yet.

"How was work?" Michael asked.

She smiled. "I took every breath."

She looked so tired.

He thought about his Jordans by the front door. He thought about how she'd been fired because he'd had the flu. He thought about gummy bears.

"What did you do today?" she asked.

"Went to the mall," he said.

"Did you buy anything?"

"I bought a book."

She raised her eyebrows. "A book?"

"Yes. It's called *Our Angry Earth*." The book was next to his portable stereo, still in the bag. "I wish you didn't have to work all the time."

"Be careful what you wish for," she said, winking. "If I wasn't at work, I'd be here, bothering you."

"That wouldn't be so bad."

"You're right. It wouldn't." She stared at him a beat longer. Then she blew him a kiss. "Sleep tight, my perfect boy."

After she closed the door, Michael pulled up his bedsheet and stared at the water stain on his ceiling.

"Paige Kaminski," he said.

He tried to think of a word that described her smile, but nothing came to him.

Maybe she thought you were cute too, Michael thought.

But that wasn't possible. No girl in the history of the world had ever liked Michael. He was too shy, too scrawny, too awkward. He was a kid who froze in front of his classmates and then asked to go to the bathroom. He was a kid who liked helping his teachers because they reminded him of his mom—tired and working hard and doing their best—but that was a bad thing. It made him a teacher's pet. A kiss-up. Sometimes other kids puckered their lips when he straightened Mrs. Schnurr's book bins or passed out papers for Mrs. Fajardo.

What girl would like a boy like him?

What would he say if he called her, anyway?

What if it was awkward and uncomfortable and he just sat there saying nothing?

No, better not to call.

He closed his eyes and rolled over to go to sleep.

21

Gummy bears were much harder to steal than canned fruit—the bags were noisy—but Michael was able to swipe a few without any problem. He was tempted to eat some when he got home, but he didn't want to break his number-one rule: *do not eat the Y2K supply*. He'd already disobeyed his mother by leaving the apartment while she was at work. He didn't want to press his luck.

When Gibby called at eleven forty-five, Michael was making a list of things he needed to add to the stash, like cereal, powdered milk, and two pocketknives.

"Ridge and I are at Beejee's," Gibby said. "Ridge is

going back in a few minutes. He wants you to come over so he can say goodbye."

"Back? You mean, back to the future?"

"Yes. He says he'll wait for you."

"Is Beejee there?"

"Of course not. Ridge will be *dematerializing* in front of our very eyes. According to him, at least. Not exactly the kind of thing Beejee needs to see." She paused. "Are you coming?"

"Yes. I just need to call Mr. Mosley and tell him I won't be here for lunch, and then I'll come over."

"Hurry up. Ridge is anxious to leave. Apparently 1999 is no longer fascinating to him."

"I'll be there in, like, five minutes," Michael said.

He left a message on Mr. Mosley's answering machine—"Hey, Mr. Mosley, I won't be home for lunch again today, but I'll come around later, okay?"—on his way out the door.

22

Ridge was in his original clothes, but he didn't look like himself. He was jumpy and nervous, pacing Beejee's living room and wringing his hands. He looked pale too.

"I should have gone right back as soon as I got here, but I wanted to see *something* before I left," he said. "I'm going to be in a monumental amount of trouble. Who knows what I'm returning to . . ."

"It'll be okay," Gibby said. She was perched on the arm of the sofa. "What's the worst that could happen?"

"Disciplinary action in front of the GSC. Revocation of my mother's scientific license. Shutdown of the lab. The end of spatial teleportation science for all eternity. Not to mention, the Saeed Theory of time travel could be wrong, and I may have inadvertently changed the course of human history while I was here, and when I get home, I'll encounter an alternate reality in which nothing from my previous life remains."

Gibby paused. "Okay, that sounds pretty bad. But I'm sure all your family cares about is your safety. They've probably been worried sick, and when you get home, they'll all celebrate."

"I wouldn't count on it," Ridge said. "They already think I'm more trouble than I'm worth."

"I'm sure that's not true," Gibby said. "Why would they think something like that?"

"Because I do things like travel back in time before the STM has been fully tested for human use," Ridge said. "Oh god. My mom is going to kill me. She's probably inventing a device *right now* so she can punish me for the rest of my life."

Gibby stood up and put her hands on Ridge's shoulders. He stopped pacing.

"It'll be okay," she said, speaking slowly, like a mother calming a child. "You just need to calm down. Right, Michael?"

Michael didn't respond. As someone with a weighted mind, he knew one thing for certain: telling someone to calm down never worked.

"Remember the Conklin Principle," Michael said instead. He stood next to Gibby. "At least one good outcome."

"One good outcome," Ridge repeated, nodding. "Right."

"The *what* principle?" Gibby said.

"Okay, okay, the Conklin Principle," Ridge muttered, pacing again. He counted off on his fingers. "I get home. Everyone's happy to see me. Nothing has changed. The GSC sees that Saeed was correct. No harm done."

"Exactly," Michael said. "It's possible, right?"

Ridge stopped where he was, several paces away, and took the EGG out of his pocket. "Yes. It's possible."

"No third-state thinking," Michael said, now that he was on a roll. "Just the here and now. First state."

"First state," Ridge said. He placed the EGG in the center of his palm.

For a moment—just a moment—Michael considered knocking him over and grabbing the sumbook, but the thought drifted away and a calm came in its place. Once Ridge was gone, he wouldn't have to think about it anymore.

"You ready?" Gibby asked.

Ridge took a deep breath. When he exhaled, he was overcome with a coughing fit.

"Yes," he said. "1999 is making me sick."

Michael and Gibby stood frozen in place. Maybe it was Michael's imagination, but it felt like the air radiated with shared nervousness, like they were both jumpy and scared, even though they were just standing there, watching and waiting. Michael hadn't realized how fast his heart was beating until that moment. *Thwack, thwack, thwack.* He almost didn't notice the smell of strawberries.

Almost.

"Thanks for everything you've done. Both of you," Ridge said. "Going to the Christiana Mall was the most exciting experience of my life." He straightened up, stood tall. "Don't freak out when I dematerialize. Okay?"

"Okay," Gibby and Michael said simultaneously.

Thwack, thwack, thwack.

Ridge pressed his thumb on the EGG.

Michael held his breath. His eyes tried to make sense of what was happening, because it didn't seem logical, but it *was* happening—Ridge was slipping in and out of focus. Static fizzled through the air. The hair on Michael's arms stood up. A faint crinkling sound floated around them.

Ridge was disappearing.

Actually disappearing.

"I wish I had a camera," Gibby whispered, her eyes transfixed. "I'm not going to believe this later."

But all Michael could think was: *I should have asked more questions. I should have forced him to tell me about Y2K. I should have—*

"Wait," Gibby said. "What's happening?"

Ridge was coming back into focus, like a hastily

reassembled puzzle. In seconds, he stood in front of them in full form, with his thumb still on the EGG.

He blinked.

He looked around. Looked at Michael. Looked at Gibby. And, finally, looked at the EGG. He stared at it for several seconds, not saying a word. Then he raised his head, slowly.

"Why am I still here?" he said.

AUDIO TRANSCRIPT

DATE
08/20/2199
LOCATION
SPATIAL TELEPORTATION SCIENCES DEPARTMENT
UNIVERSITY OF DELAWARE, RED KNOT CAMPUS
LABORATORY A2122

SUBJECTS

SABIO, MARIA (F/52YO/162CM/71KG/BRN/BRN/
IQ163), PHD, DST, CHIEF STS
SABIO, IAN (M/18YO/182CM/85KG/BRN/BRN/IQ157),
STUDENT
SABIO, SHALE (M/17YO/181CM/89KG/BLU/BRN/
IQ145), STUDENT
SABIO, BEX (NB/14YO/148CM/45KG/BLU/BRN/
IQ158), STUDENT

SABIO, BEX:
Something just happened, Mom! Something just
happened!

SABIO, MARIA:
What? What happened?

SABIO, BEX:
A blink in the code!

SABIO, MARIA:
A blink in the code? What does that mean?

SABIO, BEX:
It means—

SABIO, MARIA:
Holocom, page Ian Sabio and Shale Sabio to current location ASAP!

HOLOCOM:
Ian Sabio, please report to laboratory A2122 immediately.

HOLOCOM:
Shale Sabio, please report to laboratory A2122 immediately.

SABIO, BEX:
It means he tried the EGG! He's alive!

SABIO, MARIA:
Thank god. Thank god.

SABIO, BEX:
He's probably been trying it this whole time and it wouldn't come through. That means we're making progress on the code.

HOLOCOM:
Subject Ian Sabio will arrive in less than two minutes.

HOLOCOM:
Subject Shale Sabio will arrive in less than two minutes.

SABIO, MARIA:
I hope he's safe.

SABIO, BEX:
The archive said the coordinates were near the Fox Run apartment buildings, right?

I'm sure he's safe. It's not like he
rematerialized in a prison or something.

SABIO, MARIA:
What if he was attacked for his holodrip? He
spent four hundred credits on it and—

SABIO, BEX:
Mom. The holodrip won't even work over there.
The NTIs will see some weird kid with boring
clothes, and that's it. You've been up for more
than forty-eight hours. You're not thinking
straight. Maybe you should get a hydroboost
down the hall, or at least sleep for a bit. We
won't leave the monitors, I promise.

//ENTER SABIO, SHALE VIA WEST DOOR
//ENTER SABIO, IAN VIA WEST DOOR

SABIO, IAN:
Did you fix the coding? Is it working?

SABIO, BEX:
Not yet, but we're getting close. We got a
blink for the first time since the STM short-
circuited.

SABIO, SHALE:
A blink? What does that mean?

SABIO, BEX:
It means the EGG is trying to communicate
with the STM. It just can't get through all
the way.

SABIO, SHALE:
How do we know it's him?

SABIO, BEX:
The fail-safe, remember? The EGG will only
work with his thumbprint.

SABIO, IAN:
Thank god he's okay.

SABIO, MARIA:
We don't know for certain he's okay. We don't
know for certain.

SABIO, BEX:
Mom. The Conklin Principle. Remember?

SABIO, SHALE:
You should get some sleep, Mom. You haven't
slept at all and—

SABIO, MARIA:
I will do no such thing.

SABIO, IAN:
The information we have so far is promising.
Let's focus on that. He's alive. Nothing
has overtly changed in this timeprint, so
it doesn't appear that he's altered the
course of our futures. And the EGG is almost
working.

SABIO, BEX:
The short-circuit nearly destroyed the entire
STM, but I'm confident I'll be able to finish
this code and get it back online—another
positive.

SABIO, SHALE:
If this doesn't work, we should involve the GSC.

SABIO, MARIA:
We will do no such thing! If we involve the
GSC, they might dismantle the STM before
we get Ridge back. We have no idea what
protocols they'll demand. And then what? Your
brother is banished to the dark ages of the
twenty-first century? I don't think so. We'll
file a report with the GSC *after* Ridge is
home.

SABIO, SHALE:
What if, though?

SABIO, BEX:
What if what?

SABIO, SHALE:
What if we're not able to get him home?

SABIO, BEX:
Not an option. We're getting him home. I told
you, I'm almost done with the coding.

SABIO, IAN:
See, Mom? It will be okay.

SABIO, BEX:
It will, Mom. I've got this.

SABIO, MARIA:
Nothing will be okay until Ridge is back.
Safely. In one piece.

23

"I don't understand," Ridge said, frantic. "It's supposed to work." He pressed the EGG again, again, again. "I'm not supposed to be here!"

"It's okay," Gibby said. "Calm down—"

"I will *not* calm down!" Ridge said. His voice was throaty. He coughed. "In fact, I'm going to do the exact *opposite* of calming down. I'm going to have a full-on *freak-out*! It's supposed to work! Why doesn't it work?" His eyes were wild, panicked.

"How can we help?" Michael asked. He kept his voice even and steady. In his experience, that was the tone of voice that made people feel better. Not babysitter voice. Not teacher voice. Not angry voice. Just . . . steady.

"I don't know, I don't know." Ridge paced back and forth, back and forth, pressed the EGG, pressed the EGG.

"Help us understand how it works," Michael suggested. "Maybe that—"

"It takes years to understand the technology! I don't even understand it half the time, and I'm an actual *genius*!" Ridge dropped the EGG into his pocket and fanned his hands at his sides, like someone who had touched a hot surface and needed to cool down. His shoes dug a path into the cheap Fox Run carpet. "Okay, okay," he said. "Don't panic, Ridge. Don't panic. Think. *Think*."

"What are some reasons it might not work?" Gibby asked. Her voice was even now too. Quiet and reticent. "It might help to talk out some of the problems. That's what I do in algebra. I talk it out with myself in my room. I mean, I know this isn't like algebra. . . ."

Ridge suddenly stopped pacing, closed his eyes, and took a deep breath. Tension pushed into every corner of the room, the way it does when no one knows what to say or how to say it and everyone is waiting on someone to speak. For a moment Michael thought the EGG had activated and placed Ridge in some kind of frozen physical state between universes, but then Ridge exhaled and said, "There are several reasons it might not work."

"Let's name them," Gibby said.

"It's possible that the STM is inoperable for some reason. It's never been used before, not really, and it's just a prototype, so it's not improbable that there could be an unpredictable malfunction. A short-circuit, maybe," Ridge said.

"If that's what happened, it means it could be fixed," Michael said. "Right?"

"Right," Ridge replied. "That would be the best-case scenario, because my mom and my sibs are geniuses, so if anyone can fix it, it's them. And they have access to the brainpower of the GSC. Then again, my mom probably wouldn't want to involve the GSC. Their decisions are too unpredictable."

"Okay, so that's the best-case scenario," said Gibby. "What's the worst case?"

Ridge's face paled. "There are two. One—the STM doesn't exist anymore because I irrevocably destroyed my known course of history and it's never been invented, which means . . ."

Michael waited.

Which means . . . what?

"Which means your family may not exist anymore," Gibby completed, quietly.

Oh.

"Yes," Ridge said. "Not just my family, but everything and everyone I know, including the STM."

"But something happened when you first pressed the EGG," Michael countered. "You got all fizzy. That must mean the STM *does* still exist."

"That's what I think too. Which brings me to the second worst-case scenario," Ridge said.

"Which is?" Gibby asked.

"They deliberately deactivated the STM."

"Why would they do that?"

This time Michael knew the answer, but he didn't want to say it out loud.

"They don't want me to come back," Ridge said.

By late afternoon, a blister had formed on the soft pad of Ridge's thumb. His eyes were glassy, and he was weary on his feet. They spent more than an hour at the intersection of Fox Run and Mink, where Ridge said he had first rematerialized, hoping the proximity would influence the EGG. It didn't.

Gibby finally convinced him to go back to Beejee's and rest on the couch.

"I think you're sick," she said, pressing her hand to his forehead. "You probably caught Michael's cold."

Michael was leaning on the kitchen counter with his head in his hands.

"No, that's not possible," Ridge said. "I've never had a cold in my life. No one gets colds anymore. No one I know has ever—" He sat up and raised his hand to his throat. "Oh no."

"Oh no, what?" Gibby said.

"I'm not inoculated for anything in this century."

"It's just a cold," Gibby said. "We have all kinds of medicine. Right, Michael? Doesn't your mom have Nyquil or something?"

"Yeah, we've got all that," Michael said. The look on Ridge's face frightened him. "I'll go get it."

That's exactly what he planned to do—get the Nyquil, run back, pour it into a cup for Ridge—but when he stepped outside, Beejee was coming up the path, twirling his keys.

"What're you doing in my apartment, you little snot?" But he didn't say "snot."

Your apartment smells like dirty socks, Michael thought, and perhaps if he were bigger, stronger, older, he would have said all this, fists clenched, fight at the ready. But instead Beejee shoved him out of the way and strode to the door as Michael ran in the opposite direction, toward home. Once there, he found the Nyquil, but instead of going back right away, he sat on the wobbly stool at the counter and considered his next move.

He knew what he *should* do. Return with the medicine, as promised.

But he didn't want to.

He wasn't sure how long he sat there.

Long enough for Gibby to call and say never mind—she'd found some on her own.

24

Michael knew something was wrong as soon as he opened his eyes and saw his mother. He had a fuzzy memory of the phone ringing, and now she was sitting on the corner of his bed with her hand on his foot. Her eyes were tired—they were always tired—but they were pink and red-rimmed too. Like she'd been crying. Her hair spilled over her shoulders, which was unusual; she usually wore it in a ponytail because it was easier to work with it out of the way. Morning sunlight cast a glow across her face. She looked like a painting, almost.

"What's wrong?" Michael said. His mouth was dry. He thought of Beejee's angry face the night before. He thought of Gibby. He thought of Ridge.

He wasn't prepared when his mother said, "Mr. Mosley."

Michael sat up. "What about him?"

"He passed away last night."

Michael didn't speak a word. Then . . . "What do you mean?"

Maybe she meant something else. Maybe some people used "passed away" instead of "fell down" or "went to the hospital," and Michael just didn't know it. Maybe he'd misheard. Maybe she'd said, "I passed him on my way to work," and now she was going to clarify everything and Michael would laugh and tell Mr. Mosley about it later and he would laugh too.

"He died, honey," she said, simply. "He had a heart attack."

"Mr. Mosley?"

"Yes. Mr. Mosley."

Michael didn't move. He *couldn't* move. He stared at his mother.

Passed away? Mr. Mosley? No, that couldn't be right.

Maybe there was a mistake. Maybe it wasn't Mr. Mosley at all. There were a lot of people in the complex. It could be anyone. People made mistakes all the time.

"That's not true. I talked to him the other day," Michael said.

"I'm sorry, Michael." Her eyes pooled slowly, like a sink filling with water.

"He probably just didn't answer the door because it's Saturday and Saturday is his day off," Michael said. "He's probably just asleep—"

"Michael." She blinked, and the sink spilled over.

"But . . ." A lump had formed in Michael's throat at some point in the last three seconds, and he hadn't even noticed it. "But he's painting 3F."

He didn't know why he said that, but those were the words that came out. What he meant was: Mr. Mosley had unfinished business.

He turned away from his mother—he didn't want to see her glistening eyes—and threw himself back on the pillow. Then he shoved his hands under the covers and pushed his thumb into his palm.

"I'm going to stay home from work today," his mother said. "I don't want you to be by yourself."

He shot up again, like a cannon. "What? No!" That was the exact same thing she'd said before. *I'm going to stay home. I don't want you to be by yourself.* "You have to go to work! You have to!"

"Michael—"

"I don't need you here! I'll be fine by myself! You have to go to work or—"

"Michael, listen." She scooted up the bed so she was right next to him, close enough that he could see the streaks on her cheeks. "I'm going to stay home today."

Michael tossed the blankets over his head. He knew it was childish, but he didn't care. He didn't want to see her face. He wanted to go back to sleep, rewind to yesterday. Maybe none of this was even happening. Maybe he was in a dream right now.

"I know you can take of yourself, Michael," she said. "But I'm staying anyway."

Michael made himself as still as possible.

She sat there for a few seconds before closing the door quietly behind her.

25

Michael didn't just have a weighted mind. He had a weighted *body*. He'd never experienced grief before. He didn't know the way it pulled at all your muscles and created an anchor in the center of your chest.

He had plenty of experience with guilt, though, and that was heavy too. Guilt over getting his mom fired. Guilt over having shoes he knew they couldn't afford and loving them anyway. Guilt over the stolen cache under his bed. Guilt that he'd given Ridge his cold. And now? Guilt that he hadn't been home yesterday or the day before to eat bologna sandwiches with Mr. Mosley.

Maybe he would have noticed that Mr. Mosley wasn't right and told him to go to the doctor. Maybe he would have said something so Mr. Mosley would know how much Michael cared about him. Mr. Mosley probably thought he'd be all alone when the world came crashing down one second after midnight on January first. He didn't even know that Michael had a plan. Maybe Michael could have told him at lunch, if he'd been home, if he'd known.

All he'd done was unload the stupid dishwasher.

Michael imagined Mr. Mosley hearing his message yesterday. He imagined Mr. Mosley's face. The sandwiches in his hand, all packed up and ready to go. Mr. Mosley eating alone.

Unless—

Unless he didn't pick up the phone because—

Michael pressed the heels of his hands to his eyes.

His mom hadn't said when he died.

Michael now imagined a revised scenario. The phone ringing. Michael's voice, leaving a message. And Mr. Mosley, unmoving on the couch.

All alone.

26

Michael fell asleep at some point and woke up to the sound of voices in the living room. A ridiculous thought occurred to him: there *had* been a mistake and Mr. Mosley was here to clear everything up.

But no—it wasn't Mosley's voice. It was Gibby and Ridge, speaking to his mother. Minutes later, there were three light knocks on the door, and Gibby came into his room with Ridge right behind her. She was holding a takeout menu from his favorite Chinese restaurant.

"Your mom left some money and said we could order takeout if we wanted," Gibby said, waving the menu in the air before dropping it on the nightstand. "She says you like this place, China King."

Takeout? They'd only had takeout twice in nine months.

Michael rubbed his eyes, which felt like bricks.

"We convinced her to go to work," said Gibby. "We told her we'd stay with you. She asked who Ridge was, and I said he was Mr. Mosley's nephew. It was the first thing that came into my mind. It was the only way to explain why he looks like this."

Michael hadn't noticed before, but he noticed now: Ridge looked absolutely awful. His face was swollen and flushed. His eyes were sunken and bloodshot. He was wearing Beejee's cargo pants again and a ratty old Dave Matthews Band T-shirt.

"You look terrible," Michael said.

Ridge sat down just as Michael sat up.

"I feel terrible," Ridge said. "In every possible way."

"He's been sick," Gibby whispered, as if Ridge wasn't in direct earshot. "He has a fever of 101. I've been giving him Robitussin, Tylenol, aspirin, *everything*. But nothing works, and he's getting worse." She hugged herself and cupped her hands around her elbows. "I really think he needs to go to urgent care."

"I can't," Ridge said. He leaned back until he was practically lying on Michael's bed. "I can't go to urgent care. No doctors."

"Is it because of money?" Michael asked. "They have to take care of you even if you don't have money."

"No, it's not that," Ridge mumbled. He closed his eyes.

"I just gave him more Nyquil," Gibby explained. She lowered her voice to a whisper. "He says he can't see a doctor because he has technology in his body or something."

"Technology in his body? What, like a barcode?"

"He says it's called an elective immersive device. It's, like, a phone under your skin that creates holograms or something. I don't understand it, but it's there. I felt it, in his wrist. And it wasn't invented until the late twenty-first century, according to him, so there could be big consequences if someone finds it." She paused. "This is all too much. I think we need help."

"Maybe we can call Mr.—"

Michael stopped.

How could he have forgotten?

Gibby pulled him into a tight hug, filled with strawberries. This time, he didn't worry about the right way to hug her back.

He just did.

27

Ms. Rosario came home just after nine o'clock. Gibby had already gone home. Ridge was still asleep. Michael had made himself a nest of blankets on the floor. From this vantage point, he could see the stash under his bed—the canned and boxed goods pushed against the wall, like shadowy towers. The most recently stolen items (although he never liked to think of them as *thefts*), like the gummy bears and such, were in front. It all looked so small and inconsequential, just like he felt.

"Mr. Mosley's nephew is still here?" his mama whispered, eyeing the lump on the bed as she sat down cross-legged on the floor next to Michael.

"Yeah," Michael said. "He was upset, and then he fell

asleep. I didn't want to wake him. Is it okay if he stays a couple days?"

She looked surprised. No one had ever spent the night at their apartment before. Not this apartment or the one before that or the one before that.

"He lives with his mom, and they aren't really on speaking terms right now," Michael said. "He's going through a tough time."

It was all technically true, even if he had conveniently omitted some details.

"I hope it doesn't have anything to do with Mr. Mosley." She frowned.

"I don't think so. Just family stuff." Michael hated lying to his mother.

"I guess it's all right. I don't like the thought of you sleeping on the floor, though. The couch might be more comfortable."

"I'm okay." Michael shrugged. "I don't mind."

She ran her fingers through his hair. Michael stared at the ceiling.

"What time did it happen?" he asked.

Her hand stopped. "What time did what happen?"

"You know."

She paused. "Sometime yesterday afternoon," she said. "Mr. Ship went to check on him, and . . ."

The rest of her words drifted away.

Michael imagined the blinking red light on Mr. Mosley's answering machine.

One new message.

AUDIO TRANSCRIPT

DATE
08/21/2199
LOCATION
STATISTICS DEPARTMENT
UNIVERSITY OF DELAWARE, RED KNOT CAMPUS
VED-ACTIVATED SECURE RESEARCH BOOTH 0738

SUBJECTS

SABIO, MARIA (FACULTY ID 69230), PHD, DST,
CHIEF STS

VED:
Good morning, Dr. Maria Sabio. Please provide
data to begin statistical and hypothetical
analysis.

SABIO, MARIA:
Ved, protect this session under secure
passcode and voice identification.

VED:
Please initialize unique security passcode.

SABIO, MARIA:
2H30S7FM39.

VED:
Passcode 2H30S7FM39. Confirm?

SABIO, MARIA:
Confirmed.

VED:
This session is now secure and protected
under passcode 2H30S7FM39 with required voice
identification from Dr. Maria Sabio. Confirm?

SABIO, MARIA:
Confirmed.

VED:
Please provide data to begin statistical and
hypothetical analysis.

SABIO, MARIA:
Ved, please provide all hypotheticals
relative to the following question: What
repercussions would occur if Ridge Sabio
traveled back in time to Red Knot, Delaware,
in the 1990s and arrived safely?

VED:
More information is needed to provide
comprehensive analysis of hypothetical
scenario. Question one of fifty-seven. Please
identify "Ridge Sabio." Our records indicate
Ridge Sabio, Student, 16YO, 172CM, 73KG, son
of Dr. Maria Sabio. Confirm?

SABIO, MARIA:
Confirmed.

VED:
Noted. Question two of fifty-seven. Is Ridge
Sabio well-versed in customs and practices of
time period?

SABIO, MARIA:
Yes.

VED:
Noted. Question three of fifty-seven. Is Ridge Sabio costumed in the appropriate attire of time period?

SABIO, MARIA:
He's wearing a holodrip.

VED:
Noted. Question four of fifty-seven. Has Ridge Sabio been inoculated against disease and infection common in this time period?

SABIO, MARIA:
No.

VED:
Noted. Question five of fifty-seven. Does Ridge Sabio know how to operate any motor vehicles common in this time period?

SABIO, MARIA:
No.

VED:
Noted. Question six of fifty-seven. Does Ridge Sabio have possession of any false documentation that implies he is a Native Timeprint Inhabitant (NTI), thus providing opportunity for false NTI Social Security cards, passports—

SABIO, MARIA:
No.

VED:
Noted. Question seven of fifty-seven. Did
Ridge Sabio travel with any belongings other
than his clothing?

SABIO, MARIA:
Yes.

VED:
Please list all items.

SABIO, MARIA:

VED:
Please list all items.

SABIO, MARIA:
[INAUDIBLE]

VED:
Please list all items.

SABIO, MARIA:
He had a sumbook.

VED:
Ridge Sabio traveled with a sumbook. Confirm?

SABIO, MARIA:
Confirmed.

VED:
This information changes the quantitative
value of questioning needed to provide
comprehensive analysis of hypothetical
scenario. Confirm?

SABIO, MARIA:
Confirmed.

VED:
Question eight of eight hundred seventeen.
Did he—

SABIO, MARIA:
You've got to be kidding me.

VED:
I'm sorry, your prompt was unclear. Repeat?

SABIO, MARIA:
Never mind. Continue.

VED:
Question eight of eight hundred seventeen.
Did he travel with any documentation that
would make it possible for Native Time
Inhabitants to interpret OELC?

SABIO, MARIA:
I said he had the sumbook and that was it.

VED:
Yes or no?

SABIO, MARIA:
No.

VED:
Noted. Question nine of—

SABIO, MARIA:
Just run the hypotheticals, Ved.

VED:
Would you like to run the hypotheticals
without benefit of answering further—

SABIO, MARIA:
Yes!

VED:
Noted. Please hold for hypotheticals.

28

"**D**id you know Mr. Mosley was going to die?" Michael asked the next morning. Ridge was still in Michael's bed, and Michael was on the floor. They weren't facing each other, but Michael could tell Ridge was awake by his breathing.

"No," Ridge said. "How would I know something like that?"

"The sumbook."

Ridge was still wearing Beejee's old cargo shorts with the book tucked inside. He hadn't taken off his shirt, or his socks either. The comforter was pulled up to his chin. His voice was throaty and tired. He was holding the EGG. He'd slept with that too. Michael had woken up in the middle of the night to use the bathroom and had seen Ridge asleep, a sheen of sweat on his forehead, with his thumb resting on the scanner.

"The sumbook doesn't list everything that happens," Ridge said now. "That would be impossible."

"So it doesn't say anything about people? Just events, like the earthquake?"

"It lists *some* people. But it can't list everyone."

Michael blinked. "That's it, then? Mr. Mosley dies and he isn't even remembered? Nobody cares? No history for him?"

"Sometimes history remembers people who don't deserve it and forgets the ones who do," Ridge said. "Besides, he's being remembered right now, by you. And me. And Gibby. And your mom. Just because he isn't written down in a book doesn't mean he wasn't important."

"No, I get it. History doesn't care about maintenance men who work in apartment buildings or single moms who work three jobs. They're just . . . what? Blips."

"We're all blips, Michael," Ridge said. He coughed, then lay silent for a while. "And we're all part of history. You, me, Gibby, Mr. Mosley, your mom, my mom, even stupid Beejee."

Michael drummed his fingers against his chest.

"Can we call Gibby?" Ridge asked. "I want to ask her if she can bring me some new clothes. I'm tired of wearing this. And I'm cold."

"I might have something." Michael got up and went to his closet. "I mean, I don't have any shorts that will fit you or anything, but I might have a shirt." He rummaged around the messy pile on the floor and found an oversized Rage Against the Machine shirt he'd bought at Goodwill a few months ago. He tossed it to Ridge, along with an extra blanket.

"Thanks," Ridge said. "What's Rage Against the Machine?"

"They're a band," Michael said, returning to his spot on the floor. "And they're way better than the Backstreet Boys."

AUDIO TRANSCRIPT

DATE
08/21/2199
LOCATION
STATISTICS DEPARTMENT
UNIVERSITY OF DELAWARE, RED KNOT CAMPUS
VED-ACTIVATED SECURE RESEARCH BOOTH 0738

SUBJECTS

SABIO, MARIA (FACULTY ID 69230), PHD, DST,
CHIEF STS

VED:
Hypothetical scenario one. Our current
timeline is unaffected, as time is singular,
circular, and linear, and these events have
already unfolded, as per the Saeed Theory of
Spatial Travel.

VED:
Hypothetical scenario two. A new timeline
is created, resulting in an existence
apart from our own, as time is divergent
and heterogeneous, and though our current
timeline appears to continue unaffected,
the timeline created by Ridge Sabio diverges
from his previous path and he continues down
said path, experiencing an alternate reality
previously unfamiliar to him, as time is
linear, but neither singular nor circular, as
per the Daystrom Theory of Spatial Travel.

VED:
Hypothetical scenario three. Our current
timeline is altered in real time in ordinary

and extraordinary ways, dependent on the actions of Ridge Sabio; contemporary Native Timeprint Inhabitants are aware of, and confused by, the changes, which could result in one, more, or all of the following—disappearance of loved ones, disappearance of self, erasure or revision of modern technology, shifts in culture, shifts in sociopolitical and economic landscape, and so on—as time is singular, yet not linear nor circular, as per the Huss-Roat Theory of Spatial Travel.

VED:
Hypothetical scenario four. Our current timeline is altered in real time in profound and ordinary ways, dependent on the actions of Ridge Sabio; contemporary Native Timeprint Inhabitants are unaware of the changes, which could result in one, more, or all of the following—disappearance of loved ones, disappearance of self, erasure or revision of modern technology, shifts in culture, shifts in sociopolitical and economic landscape, and so on—as time is singular and linear, yet not circular, as per the Noonian Theory of Spatial Travel.

VED:
Hypothetical scenario five. Ridge Sabio is unable to return to our current timeline as a result of failed rematerialization during the—

SABIO, MARIA:
Ved, how many hypothetical scenarios are there?

VED:
There are 2,017 hypothetical scenarios.

SABIO, MARIA:

VED:
Would you like me to continue?

29

Michael and Ridge slept most of Sunday away, and Michael could have continued sleeping through Monday, but there was pounding at the apartment door just after ten-thirty a.m. His eyes opened slowly as he tried to make sense of the sound. It wasn't a regular knock. This was angry and purposeful—*THUMPTHUMPTHUMPTHUMPTHUMPTHUMP*. The way police officers and SWAT teams knocked on doors on television.

He stood up and pulled on his clothes. Ridge was asleep with the EGG still in his hand. The cargo shorts were folded under his head, on the pillow.

THUMPTHUMPTHUMPTHUMPTHUMP!

He stepped slowly down the hall and toward the door, heart pounding.

What if it *was* the police?

He stood on his toes and looked through the peephole.

"I know you're there!" Beejee yelled. "Open this freaking door!"

Except he didn't say "freaking."

Blood rushed to Michael's ears. Every nerve in his body jumped.

THUMPTHUMPTHUMPTHUMPTHUMP!

"I know you're there!" Beejee yelled again. "Open up *now* or I'm calling the police!"

The police?

Shouldn't Michael be the one calling the police?

Michael turned the latch and opened the door, just a crack.

"What's the matter?" Michael asked. He hated how small his voice sounded.

Beejee pushed his way into the apartment, his head swiveling this way and that, as if he was looking for a stowaway. Then he stopped in the middle of the living room and poked his index finger into Michael's chest.

"You stole my tools!" Beejee said. "Where are they?"

Michael shrank to the size of a grape. Beejee loomed over him.

"I don't—I didn't—I don't know what you're talking about." Michael's voice caught in his throat, like he was going to cry.

Oh, god. *You can't cry. You can't cry.*

He wished Mr. Mosley were here. He wished he was as big as Jamar. He wished he was a Siberian tiger. He wished he had an EGG and could disappear to another universe. He wished he was anyone else, anywhere else.

Beejee strode down the short hall, straight to Michael's bedroom, where Ridge was sitting up, eyes rimmed with red.

"What's going on?" Ridge asked.

"This kid stole my tools!" Beejee said. And now he was in Michael's room, opening the door to his closet, peeking under the nightstand.

Ridge locked eyes with Michael. A question.

Michael stood in the doorway, frozen. He felt his heart beat in his chest, in his stomach, in his head, in his feet. He pressed his thumb into his palm again and again and again. He tried to take a deep breath, but he couldn't move. He'd transformed into concrete. No, not concrete. Glass. Something solid, but easily broken.

Beejee dropped to his knees and craned his head under the bed. Ridge got up, out of his way.

Michael swallowed.

He couldn't breathe.

Just like that, Beejee found his pliers and hammer. He scooped them out with one oversized hand, then stood at full height, eyes blazing at Michael.

"You dirty thief!" Beejee yelled, waving the tools in the air.

Michael imagined Beejee bringing the hammer down on his head. Pulling out his hair with the pliers. Pummeling him into the ground, just like he'd done to that guy in the parking lot that time. Each of the scenarios clicked through his mind. *Click, click, click.*

When Beejee took an enormous step forward, two things happened simultaneously: Michael took a step back, cowering, and Ridge moved in front of him.

"It was me!" Ridge said, waving his hands in the air. "It wasn't Michael. It was me. I stole your stuff."

"You little—"

"I was going to return them," Ridge said. "I just needed to borrow—um . . ." He eyed the tools. Michael saw the gears turning in his head, trying to identify what kind of tools they were. ". . . a screwdriver and a wrench, maybe?"

Beejee closed the gap between them. He was practically nose to nose with Ridge now. Or nose to hairline, as the case may be.

"Do *not* step a *foot* back in my apartment again," Beejee said. He shoved Ridge away, and in one giant swoop, he moved to the bed and grabbed his old cargo shorts too. "And you can't borrow any more of my *stuff*!"

Except he didn't say "stuff."

Ridge's eyes widened. "Wait! Let me get my things out of the pockets!"

But Beejee had already pushed his way past them and out of the room.

"Consider it my payment!" he yelled.

"Wait!" Ridge ran a few steps forward but stopped, teetering on his feet. He looked like he was about to faint. Michael watched him, wondering what he should do if Ridge *did* faint. He looked so, so sick. "I have to—" Ridge stumbled ahead, clutching the wall for balance.

"I'll get it," Michael said quickly. "I'll get your book, I promise! Wait here. I'll be right back. Don't worry!"

He turned and ran after Beejee.

30

"I really think he needs to go to a hospital," Gibby said that night, as she and Michael sat side by side on the couch. Ridge remained in bed, drowsy and running a high fever—102 degrees, in fact. "What if he gets worse and worse?"

Michael stared at his Jordans, sitting obediently by the door.

I don't know, he thought. *I don't know.*

"I can't believe Beejee acted like such a maniac," Gibby continued. "And why did Ridge steal that stuff in the first place? He said he was just curious about antiquated tools, but I don't know. Maybe the fever is making him hallucinate or something. What do you think?"

I don't know, Michael thought.

"I'm going to check the dumpster again in the morning, when Mr. Ship won't see me," she said. "Do you think Beejee's lying? He said he threw it in there, but I don't know. What if he kept it?" When Michael didn't reply, she continued, "I don't know. I don't think he did. I mean, for all he knows, it's just a book. And lord knows he doesn't read. We'll just have to take his word for it. What choice do we have? I'm going back in the morning to search. Maybe around seven or seven thirty. You should meet me there to help look."

"Okay," he said.

She grabbed his hand loosely and turned toward him. "I know you're upset that you weren't able to get it back, but the fact that you went after him makes you a bad-A," she said. "Beejee can be really scary, and Ridge said you were terrified."

She released his hand.

Michael wondered what he had looked like for Ridge to say that. He *was* terrified, of course. He just wasn't aware that he *looked* terrified.

Michael's heart thundered, thinking about everything now. Beejee's eyes when Michael had followed him out into the courtyard and yelled his name. Beejee's fist when he'd grabbed Michael's shirt and shoved him to the side. Beejee's long strides as he walked toward the dumpster.

Michael wanted this conversation to be over as soon as possible.

"My mom will be home any minute," he said. "You can go home if you want. I'm about to go to bed anyway, and it's not a babysitting day."

"Are you sure?"

"Yeah. I'm sure."

Gibby sighed and glanced toward Michael's bedroom door. "What are we going to do about Ridge, though?"

"I'll talk to my mom," Michael said. "I won't tell her everything. I'll just tell her he's sick and needs to go to the hospital."

"What if she asks about his family?"

"I don't know." For the first time in his life, he wanted Gibby to leave, get out, go home. "I'll figure it out. I'm tired."

Gibby waited a few beats, then said, "Okay. Meet me at the dumpster tomorrow morning, though. Okay? Seven thirty."

Michael nodded but didn't say another word.

Fifteen minutes later, Michael's mother walked through the door carrying something—no, *somethings*—under her arm.

"I didn't expect to see you there, sitting on the couch in silence," she said, smiling. She kicked the door closed behind her just as Michael stood up to help. "I have something for you."

She was holding a jar, he saw now. It was blue plastic, so

he couldn't see what was inside. And she also had Gibby's Christopher Pike book, of all things.

She kicked off her shoes, perched on the wobbly stool, and placed everything on the countertop. Michael eyed the items curiously. There was a strip of tape on the outside of the jar with his name on it. MICHAEL ROSARIO, written in Mr. Mosley's identifiable, all-caps print.

"What's this?" he asked.

"Mr. Ship is cleaning out Mr. Mosley's apartment," she said. "He found these things and told me to pass them along. There was this jar with your name on it. And this book, apparently, which has Gibby's name in it."

Michael leaned toward the jar. "What's in there?"

"I have no idea. I didn't open it." She brushed a strand of hair away from her face. "Mr. Ship said you can walk through Mr. Mosley's apartment if you want, once it's ready for all the pickups."

"What pickups?"

"He's donating just about everything."

Michael lifted the jar, carefully. It didn't weigh much.

He shook it.

Something papery moved inside.

Then he remembered the conversation he'd had with Mr. Mosley last week.

I had a good mama, like you. She'd take out money from every paycheck and drop it in a big jar with my name on it. Michael unscrewed the lid and peered inside.

Sure enough: money. Bundled in a rubber band. He couldn't see the denominations, but there were several bills. Maybe forty or so.

It was only a few hundred bucks.

"It's money," Michael said.

And then—although he hadn't expected it and wasn't the least bit prepared to stop it from happening—a flood of tears suddenly pushed its way up, up, up, from the bottom of his chest to the center of his throat, and now to his eyes. He blinked them away and put the lid on top of the jar again.

"A few hundred bucks," he said. He pushed the jar toward her. "I want you to have it. For bills."

She pushed it back. "Absolutely *not*. This has *your* name on it. Not mine."

"But . . ."

"No buts. It's out of the question." She stood up and crossed her arms. "I'll help you figure out how to spend it *responsibly*, but I won't take a dime and you won't bring it up again. Understood?"

Michael swallowed. Sniffled.

But I don't deserve it, Mama. I don't deserve it.

"All you have to do is say thank you," she said. She pressed her palms together and lifted her chin to the ceiling, as if Mr. Mosley's spirit was floating above their apartment.

Who knows, maybe it was.

Michael looked up too.

"Thank you," he said.

AUDIO TRANSCRIPT

DATE
08/25/2199
LOCATION
SPATIAL TELEPORTATION SCIENCES DEPARTMENT
UNIVERSITY OF DELAWARE, RED KNOT CAMPUS
LABORATORY A2122

SUBJECTS

SABIO, MARIA (F/52YO/162CM/70KG/BRN/BRN/
IQ163), PHD, DST, CHIEF STS
SABIO, IAN (M/18YO/182CM/86KG/BRN/BRN/IQ158), STUDENT
SABIO, SHALE (M/17YO/181CM/89KG/BLU/BRN/
IQ159), STUDENT
SABIO, BEX (F/14YO/148CM/46KG/BLU/BRN/IQ160), STUDENT

SABIO, BEX:
I think I got it, Mom. The one was inverted
and the two zeros here were running
concurrently instead of consecutively. I
reversed the code. Let's try it now.

SABIO, MARIA:
Ian, attempt to repower the STM again.

SABIO, IAN:
Confirmed. Repowering the STM.

//STM1 INITIATING
//STM1 MALFUNCTION

SABIO, IAN:
It didn't work! I can't believe it didn't work!
Now what. And where's Shale? Why isn't he here?

SABIO, MARIA:
He's preparing the report for the GSC.

SABIO, IAN:
I thought you said we weren't involving them.

SABIO, MARIA:
We've been trying to fix the STM for days
and nothing's working. With their collective
knowledge, they might see something we can't
see.

SABIO, IAN:
What happens if their recommendation is
to dismantle the STM and leave Ridge out
there? A lot of their theories of time don't
coincide with—

SABIO, MARIA:
I know, I know. But we have to take the
chance. The window is closing. I don't know
what's right or wrong anymore. I just want
him home.

SABIO, IAN:
They're going to revoke your license.

SABIO, MARIA:
That's going to happen anyway. What
difference does it make if it's now or later?
Besides, I don't care about the license. All
I care about is getting him home.

SABIO, IAN:
Let me take the blame, Mom. I'll say it was
my fault somehow. I'll tell them—

SABIO, BEX:
I think I got it, Mom.

SABIO, IAN:
That's what you said last time.

SABIO, BEX:
I mean it. I found another set of degraded
codes and reversed them. I really think it
will work this time.

SABIO, MARIA:
My heart can't handle all these false starts.

SABIO, IAN:
The Conklin Principle, Mom. Positive outcome—
he comes back. *Today.*

SABIO, MARIA:

SABIO, IAN:
Right, Mom?

SABIO, MARIA:
Okay. Attempt to repower the STM. Again.

SABIO, BEX:
Repowering the STM.

//STM1 INITIATING
//STM1 INITIATING
//STM1 INITIATING
//STM1 ACTIVE

31

The rain woke Michael. *Pitter-pat, pitter-pat, pitter-pat.* He rubbed his eyes, sat up, and stretched. Every bone in his body ached. His head hurt too, from all the crying, which he'd done quietly until he fell asleep. His face itched and his pillow was damp.

He got up and used the toilet. He studied his hands as he washed them, imagining picking through the dumpster with Gibby. He didn't want to go. There was no point. And he didn't want to look Gibby in the face, either. *Beejee can be really scary and Ridge said you were terrified.*

Plus he'd have to tell Gibby that he hadn't talked to his mom about Ridge after all. *I decided to wait one more day,* he would tell her. *I don't want to give her more to worry about.* And it was true. But it was also true that Ridge absolutely, positively did *not* want to go to the hospital, and Michael didn't feel right about forcing the issue.

Then again, Ridge couldn't stay in his room forever.

It was all too much to think about, to be honest.

He splashed water on his face and wandered into the living room. It was fifteen minutes after seven; his mother's presence still hung in the air.

The jar sat on the counter. Michael imagined Mr. Mosley cutting the strip of masking tape and writing MICHAEL ROSARIO on it, thinking, *Michael Rosario is a good kid. He deserves this.*

But he didn't *feel* like a good kid.

He felt like a thief.

He grabbed Pop-Tarts out of the cabinet, took the jar and Gibby's book from the counter, and returned to his room. He sat on the floor with the jar in front of him and the packet dangling from his teeth. He opened the book where it'd been dog-eared. Page 132, Chapter VIII. "The rain was still coming down the following Monday morning," the first line read.

Mr. Mosley had made it all the way to page 132.

Ridge's breaths rattled from the bed.

"Is it raining?" Ridge said, eyes still closed. "I hear rain."

Michael set the book aside and let the Pop-Tarts fall to

the carpet. "I guess it still rains in the future, then?"

"There is always rain. Life can't exist without rain." Ridge sat up, the EGG still clutched in his hand. "It's good that it's raining."

"Good? Why?"

"The sumbooks can't survive water."

Michael was in the process of unscrewing the jar, but he stopped. "Really? Why not?"

"One of my mom's fail-safes, just in case it has to be destroyed in a hurry."

Ridge's neck was splotchy and crimson. He looked like he'd lost fifteen pounds overnight.

"When was the last time you ate?" Michael asked. Michael had intended to eat the Pop-Tarts himself, but from the looks of things, Ridge needed them more.

"I don't know."

"You should eat these Pop-Tarts," Michael said. He scooped them up and tossed the packet to Ridge. Then he opened the jar, dumped the money on the floor, and pulled the rubber band off. It took a moment for what he was seeing to click into place in his brain.

Wait.

No, this couldn't be right.

He'd expected them to all be one-dollar bills. Tens, at the most.

But these were all hundred-dollar bills.

Each and every one of them.

Ridge squinted at the money. "What's all that?"

"Money," Michael said. "Mr. Mosley left it for me."

He counted the bills. There were fifty of them.

"It's five thousand dollars," Michael said, breathless.

"Five thousand dollars," Ridge repeated. "Is that a lot?"

Michael could hardly speak. "Yes."

Ridge nodded. He didn't seem very impressed. Maybe five thousand dollars wasn't much money in the twenty-second century, but in 1999, it was a fortune.

"What am I going to do with all this?" Michael asked.

A million scenarios ran through his head. The next pair of Jordans would drop later this year—he could get a second pair. And a new wardrobe too. No more secondhand clothes. He could buy Gibby all the books she wanted. And he'd pay off all their bills, even if his mom refused. He could get a new stash. A *proper* stash. One that filled his entire closet, maybe his entire room. When Y2K came, they'd be ready.

He could give some to Ridge, just in case he never made it home. Ridge would need money to survive without a family. Maybe he and his mom could become Ridge's family. They could adopt him, and then Michael would have a brother and he wouldn't be alone so much, especially now that Mr. Mosley was gone, and maybe Ridge could give him more advice about girls and going to school, and maybe Ridge could help him practice in case he really *did* decide to go out for football—

"What is a Pop-Tart?" Ridge said.

Michael's mind was spinning so fast, the question barely registered.

"Michael?" Ridge repeated. "What is a Pop-Tart?"

"It's a breakfast thing."

"I don't know if I'll be able to eat this. My throat is on fire. It hurts to even talk." He paused. "You should save the money for college. You still have to pay for college in the twentieth century, right? And it's only going to get more and more expensive until finally . . ."

Michael looked up. "Until finally, what?"

"Never mind."

"College. That seems so far away."

"You could invest it."

"Invest it? I don't know anything about that stuff. I don't even know how it works."

"You invest five thousand now, you can have five times that amount in a few years."

"Or I could have nothing."

"Not knowing is part of life."

Michael stared at the money.

Ridge stared at the Pop-Tarts.

"Gibby really thinks we need to take you to a hospital,"

Michael said. He gathered the bills slowly and returned them to the jar. "Like, today. You're getting worse."

Ridge cupped the EGG in his hands. "I don't care if I get better or not," Ridge said. His voice was strained and strange, not at all the way it had sounded when he first arrived. "I've never been sick before, and I'll probably die, but it doesn't matter."

Michael didn't move a muscle.

"I deserve only bad things," Ridge continued. "Being sick. The EGG not working. Losing my family."

Michael frowned. "No, you don't."

"Yes, I do. It was stupid, what I did."

"Everyone makes mistakes," Michael said quietly. "It doesn't mean you deserve only bad things."

Ridge hung his head and stared at his hands. "I just want to fall asleep and never wake up. I deserve—"

Ridge furrowed his eyebrows, staring at the EGG.

"Ridge?"

"Michael."

Michael stood up.

He saw it right away.

The light on the EGG was on.

And it was bright green.

32

Michael's sneakers splashed through the puddles as he dashed across the courtyard. The rain was gentle but steady, falling on his shoulders, his hair, his arms. He couldn't remember the last time he'd run this fast. It felt good, like energy shooting through his body, like he could run forever. His body had been so heavy these past few days, but at this moment, it felt light. Not free, exactly—the image of Mr. Mosley writing his name on a slip of tape still lingered in his mind, even now, as he ran—but awake and alive.

Gibby was standing near the dumpster. She saw him coming and raised her hand in a gentle wave, but a flash of confusion crossed her face; she'd been expecting him, but she hadn't expected him to be *running*.

He came to a stop in front of her and leaned forward to catch his breath.

"It's on," he said, gasping, gasping. "The EGG is on."

It took a moment for this to register, but when it did, she took off running too.

33

Gibby stopped at her apartment to grab Ridge's holodrip, which she'd kept safely tucked in her closet, before they returned to Michael's apartment. Ridge was so tired and weak, he needed Michael's help to change into it, and when they leaned against each other, Ridge's fever burned through Michael's skin.

"Will they be able to make you better when you get there?" Michael asked.

"Yes," he said. "All it will take is a patch."

And now they were in Michael's room, standing in a triangle, staring at each other. Michael held his breath and waited for Ridge to say something.

"Do you have something I can write on?" Ridge asked.

"Like paper?" Michael said.

"Yes. Anything will do. And something to write with."

Gibby snatched the China King takeout menu from the nightstand as Michael hurried into the kitchen for the pen his mama used for making grocery lists and writing checks.

Ridge turned the menu over, wrote something in the corner, then tore it off, folded it in three, and handed it to Michael.

"Don't look at it yet," Ridge said. "And keep it someplace safe."

"Okay," Michael said. He shoved it in his pocket.

"I want to give you something," Gibby said quickly. "Like, a memento. I should have grabbed something when I was at home, but I forgot. You need something to take back with you, right? A souvenir or something!"

"I don't need anything," Ridge said. "I just want you to promise me that you'll destroy the sumbook if you find it. The repercussions are—"

"This!" she blurted out suddenly, grabbing her book from the floor. "Take this!" She nudged it into Ridge's chest, forcing him to take it. Before he could say anything else, Gibby started talking again, her voice pitched and excited. "We need something to remember you too! Otherwise I'll never believe this happened! It doesn't have to be something that will break the universe or whatever. Just something simple. Here!" She picked up the takeout menu, which now had a corner missing, and waved it in his face. "Write your name on this. Nothing else. That won't hurt anything, right?"

Ridge hesitated. "I guess not." He tucked the book under his arm and wrote his name down. His movements were slow and sluggish, so the letters wavered a bit, but once he'd finished, there it was. RIDGE, in all caps, clear as day.

He put the pen aside.

"Thank you," Gibby said. She took the paper in both hands carefully.

Something in Ridge's eyes flickered at that moment.

"What's the matter?" Gibby asked. "You have a weird look on your face."

Ridge looked at Michael, and Michael's mind backtracked to the day after they'd visited the mall, when they sat on the couch side-by-side, watching Ricki Lake.

It's really annoying being named after a piece of paper.

Ridge glanced down at the Christopher Pike book. He opened it to the first page. Gibby's name was written on the inside of the cover, in black ink. ELIZABETH GIBSON. His mouth formed a perfect circle.

"I thought your name was Gibby," Ridge said.

"It is. It's a nickname. Why?" She glanced between Ridge and Michael. She didn't see Ridge shake his head and put his finger to his lips.

Michael nodded, imperceptibly.

"Is something wrong?" Gibby asked. "What's going on?"

"No. Nothing's wrong." Ridge slipped the book into his back pocket, where the sumbook had once lived, and took out the EGG.

Gibby held the menu to her chest. "I guess this is it."

Ridge's thumb hovered over the EGG. "There's a chance it still won't work. The light doesn't necessarily mean anything."

"It'll work," Michael said.

"Thank you both," Ridge said. "For helping me."

"How will we know you made it home safely?" Gibby asked.

"You won't," Ridge said.

"Not knowing is part of life," Michael said.

There was more he wanted to say—about the sumbook, about the first state, about everything. He wanted to tell Ridge that Michael and his mama would have taken care of him if he'd been trapped, that he would have been okay, that he didn't need to wish to never wake up again. Instead, he said, "I'm the one who stole Beejee's tools."

He didn't say it to either of them in particular. He spoke it to the room.

Gibby's head snapped in his direction. "Wait, what?"

"I took them for my Y2K stash."

"Stash? What—"

"Everyone makes mistakes," Ridge said. "It doesn't mean they deserve only bad things."

Michael had more to confess—his tongue suddenly wanted to share all his secrets—but Ridge was already fading. A flicker at first, like before—a faint quiver you'd miss if you blinked. But then it steadied, and soon Ridge looked like a program that was about to go off the air. Michael wanted to reach out, touch the moving particles, but he didn't dare.

The air filled with static.

The hair on Michael's arms lifted. But, just as quickly, the feeling was gone—and so was Ridge.

The room was silent and still.

Michael and Gibby stood there frozen for what felt like a thousand years.

"Do you think anything changed?" Gibby said. "I mean . . . do you think he ruined the timeline, being here? Or maybe *we* messed it up too?"

"No. I think everything happened just the way it was supposed to."

Ridge's departure hung in the air between them.

Neither of them knew what to say.

Michael pulled the note from his pocket and unfolded it.

"What does it say?" Gibby asked.

"Netflix IPO 2002."

"Netflix? Like that DVD thing?"

Michael shrugged. "I guess."

"What is IPO?"

"I have no idea." Michael lifted the Waldenbooks bag from its half-forgotten spot on the floor and pulled *Our Angry Earth* out of it. He opened it to a random place and stuck the slip of paper inside.

"I wonder if Mr. Mosley read my book," Gibby said quietly.

"He got to page one thirty-two," Michael said, thinking of the dog-eared page.

Gibby's eyes glistened with unshed tears. Michael wondered if she was crying for Ridge, Mr. Mosley, or both.

"Do you think Ridge made it home?" she said.

"Yes," Michael said. "But I guess we'll never know for sure."

Not knowing might be part of life, but that didn't make it any easier.

AUDIO TRANSCRIPT

DATE
08/24/2199
LOCATION
SPATIAL TELEPORTATION SCIENCES DEPARTMENT
UNIVERSITY OF DELAWARE, RED KNOT CAMPUS
LABORATORY A2122

SUBJECTS

SABIO, MARIA (F/52YO/162CM/70KG/BRN/BRN/
IQ163), PHD, DST, CHIEF STS
SABIO, IAN (M/18YO/182CM/86KG/BRN/BRN/IQ157),
STUDENT
SABIO, SHALE (M/17YO/181CM/89KG/BLU/BRN/
IQ145), STUDENT
SABIO, RIDGE (M/16YO/172CM/68KG/BRN/BRN/
IQ160), STUDENT
SABIO, BEX (NB/14YO/148CM/46KG/BLU/BRN/
IQ158), STUDENT

//ENTER SABIO, RIDGE VIA STM1

SABIO, MARIA:
Oh my god! Oh my god!

//INITIALIZING STM1 DETOX PROCEDURE

SABIO, SHALE:
Ridge, can you hear us?

SABIO, BEX:
Of course he can't hear us. The STM is
soundproof.

SABIO, IAN:
Now is not the time for—

SABIO, MARIA:
Something's wrong with him. He looks pale.
How do you open the door to this thing?
Someone open the door!

SABIO, IAN:
You're the one who designed it, Mom.

SABIO, BEX:
The door will open when the detox procedure
is over, remember?

SABIO, SHALE:
He's trying to tell us something.

SABIO, BEX:
Why am I the only one who understands the
concept of soundproofing?

//STM1 DETOX PROCEDURE COMPLETE

SABIO, MARIA:
The doors are opening, thank god. Ridge!
Ridge! Someone get the HUCK!

SABIO, SHALE:
I'll get it.

SABIO, MARIA:
Your skin is so warm! What happened? What
happened?

SABIO, RIDGE:
I caught a cold.

SABIO, MARIA:
Your brother is getting the HUCK. Don't
worry, okay?

SABIO, BEX:
Shale, hurry up!

SABIO, SHALE:
I'm moving as fast as I can!

SABIO, RIDGE:
I lost the sumbook, Mom. I lost the sumbook.

SABIO, SHALE:
Here's the HUCK. Put it on his arm.

SABIO, BEX:
You lost the sumbook?

SABIO, IAN:
Wait—you lost the sumbook?

SABIO, RIDGE:
Someone took it . . . but it was raining . . .
I'm sorry, Mom. I'm sorry—

SABIO, MARIA:
Shh, shh. It's okay. Just be quiet for a few
minutes and wait for the HUCK to kick in. I
don't care about the sumbook right now, okay?

SABIO, SHALE:
This is by far the dumbest thing you've ever done.

SABIO, MARIA:
Shale! This is *not* the time.

SABIO, SHALE:
Now that he's alive and safe, I am well within my right to tell him what an idiot he is.

SABIO, BEX:
Is the HUCK working yet?

SABIO, MARIA:
The HUCK says his fever is down to ninety-nine.

SABIO, RIDGE:
Did anything change, Mom? Did anything change?

SABIO, MARIA:
Nothing changed.

SABIO, SHALE:
If Noonian is correct, then things may have changed and we're not aware of it.

SABIO, MARIA:
Not helping.

SABIO, IAN:
Everything is just as you left it, Ridge.

SABIO, BEX:
We were *so* scared. Even Shale. He barely slept.

SABIO, SHALE:
Not true! I slept soundly.

SABIO, IAN:
If you don't have the sumbook, what's in your
pocket?

SABIO, RIDGE:
A memento.

SABIO, BEX:
Final Act by Christopher Pike? What kind of
book is this?

SABIO, IAN:
Oh my god! Mom! Mom! Look at the name inside!
Elizabeth Gibson!

SABIO, SHALE:
Elizabeth Gibson?

SABIO, MARIA:
Ridge! Elizabeth Gibson?

SABIO, BEX:
But it can't be the *actual* Elizabeth Gibson,
can it? Wait . . . can it?

SABIO, IAN:
You met *the actual* Elizabeth Gibson?

SABIO, BEX:
Oh my god. Did you tell her you were from the
future? You didn't, did you? Oh my god. Did
you?

SABIO, SHALE:
He did. I know he did. He told her. You did,
didn't you? How can you be so—

SABIO, RIDGE:
I had to. And I didn't even know her real
name until five minutes ago.

SABIO, BEX:
Technically, two hundred years ago.

SABIO, MARIA:
According to the Saeed Theory, all this has
already happened. So it's very likely that
Ridge's interactions with her are what led
to the founding in the first place. Ridge,
you're all better now, yes? Good. Let's get
you some food. You can tell us everything
while we eat. Can you stand up?

SABIO, IAN: What was she like, Ridge?

SABIO, BEX: Was she solving equations every
five seconds and rattling off all incredible
philosophies? Did she keep a notebook full of
complicated diagrams?

SABIO, RIDGE:
No. She was just . . . Gibby.

SABIO, BEX:
And?

SABIO, RIDGE:
She likes mystery novels.

SABIO, IAN:
And?

SABIO, RIDGE:
She has a car named Eloise.

SABIO, SHALE:
And?

SABIO, RIDGE:
And she has terrible taste in music.

34

It was strange, the way a space could stay the same and change all at once.

Mr. Mosley's apartment was just as it had always been—same furniture, same knick-knacks, same DVDs—but everything was different. The DVDs were stacked on the floor next to the entertainment center, waiting to be hauled away. His clothes were neatly folded in bins. The contents of his kitchen—canned goods, six-packs of Dr Pepper, unopened bags of Lay's—sat in boxes next to the front door. There were odd things here and there. An electric razor. A Philadelphia Eagles wallet. Cheap old watches that ticked on and on without him.

Michael scanned the room as his mama sorted through

the DVDs to find *Raising Arizona*. Mr. Mosley always insisted they keep it, but she'd make Michael return it every time. "When we watch it now, it will remind us of him," she'd said on their way over.

Mr. Ship said they could take anything they wanted before he donated everything, but Michael didn't know where to begin. He didn't want *things*. He wanted Mr. Mosley. And none of these items would bring him back.

His eyes landed on the box of canned goods.

"I'll take those," he said, pointing at them.

His mama had found the DVD. She clutched it to her chest and retraced her steps to see what he was pointing at.

"The canned goods?" she said, raising her eyebrows.

"Yes. The canned goods."

"Why would you want canned goods? We have plenty."

"For my stash."

"Your stash? What stash?"

"Oh. I mean, I don't have a stash or anything," Michael said quickly. "But I want to start one. For Y2K. You know, just in case."

She stared at the canned goods, then turned toward him. "Michael, you don't need a stash."

"How do you know? You have no idea what's going to happen. The news says—"

"If you want a stash, we can sit down and discuss it.

Maybe we can talk about using part of your money to start one. Canned goods and bottled water aren't very expensive, and you're a rich man now, right?" She bumped his arm.

Why didn't anyone take Y2K seriously?

"I think we should take the canned goods," Michael said. "It's practical. And you never know if we'll have enough. We might—"

"Michael," she said, her voice soft, but serious. "We have plenty of canned goods. And we can buy more if we need to. I know we're not Rockefellers, but we can afford canned goods. There are some people who can't. Don't you think they might need this food more than us?"

Well, yes, Michael thought. *But—*

"Besides," she continued. "Mr. Ship said you should take something to remember Mr. Mosley by. A memento. Canned goods aren't much of a memento, are they?"

"I don't need a memento because I'm not going to forget him."

"I know you won't forget, honey, but sometimes it's nice to have something that once belonged to someone you loved. Then you can think of them every time you see it." She tapped the DVD. "Or watch it."

"We can take the canned goods *and* I'll take a memento."

"We're leaving the canned goods for someone who really needs them, Michael. If you don't want a memento, you don't have to take one. But we're not hauling canned goods out of here—not when they're supposed to go to a food pantry, for people who really need them."

Michael shifted from foot to foot. He felt defensive and irritated all of a sudden, like he was doing something wrong.

Was he?

Was it wrong to want the canned goods?

"It's *my* job to take care of *you*," his mama said. "Remember that, okay?"

Michael paused. "Okay."

It's good to be taken care of sometimes. It's the way it ought to be.

35

Beejee was many things, but he was not a liar. He'd thrown the sumbook in the dumpster, just like he said.

Michael saw the whole thing.

Beejee had stormed out of the Rosarios' apartment. Michael raced after him, calling his name. Beejee turned around, eyes on fire, then grabbed Michael by the shirt and shoved him to the side. At first, Michael couldn't move. Couldn't speak. So Beejee kept walking, not realizing that Michael was still behind him—stealthy, like the stray cats he loved so much.

Michael watched Beejee stop between buildings to rifle through the pockets of the cargo shorts. Looking for money, no doubt. He didn't care one bit about the book. He threw it. The book made an arc in the air and landed in the garbage without a sound. Three minutes later, Beejee was back in his apartment and Michael was reaching into the dumpster.

He retrieved the book easily.

He slipped it into the waistband of his shorts.

"I couldn't stop him, Ridge," Michael said when he got home. "I'm sorry. He wouldn't give it back. I tried to stop him, but—"

"Call Gibby," Ridge had said, frantic. "She'll get it. She has to. She has to—"

But now here it was, on Michael's bed, staring back at him.

He hadn't opened it. Not once. Not yet.

Sometimes it had felt like there was a magnet in his room instead of a book—it pulled and pulled. The pull was so strong, he could barely fight it. But he'd been patient. He'd waited for the right moment. *This* moment. He was alone. His breaths were steady and even. He was mentally prepared.

At least he thought he was.

His heart pounded so loudly, it hurt.

Thwack, thwack, thwack.

His body was still on the outside. Twitchy on the inside.

He pinched the bottom corner of the cover.

He opened the book.

What Michael Saw

YZ2ØK/,A.ZK.ØA.Z"TZHØE/ZMØIZLZLØEZN/
NZIZUØM/BØUZGZ"O/RØ"ZT/HØEZY/EØAZR/
Ø2#0Z0#0ZPØR/O#BØL/E#M/,"ZRZEZFZEZRZSØT#O/
AØWZO/RØL#D#W#I/DØEZP/AZNØI#CZTØH/
AØTZOØC#CZUZR/RZEØD#O/NØW#O/RØL/
DØAZSZTZHZEZC/A/L#EØNZDZAZRN/EØAØRØE#D/
JZAZNZUZAZRØY/1Ø2#0Ø0/0/AZTZØT#H/
ETZIZMZEØ,/I/TW#A/SØB/EØL#I/E/VZEØDØT/H/
A#T#W/O/RØL#D/WØI#D/EZCØO/M#P#/UZT/E/
RØS/Y/S/T/E/M/S/WZOZUZLZDZMZAZLØF/
U#NØC/T#I#O#N/WZHZEZN/IØN#T/E#RØN/
AØL#PZRZOZGZRZAZM/S#Y/S/TZEØM/S#RZEØSØE/
TØT#O/TZHZE/YØE#AØR/0Z0

36

Michael blinked. He narrowed his eyes, as if the page was simply out of focus. He turned one page, then another and another, hoping he would see one sentence, one *word*, that he understood. Anything familiar. But each block of text was as foreign as the next. It was all gibberish. Ridge had lied—this wasn't a real book. This was nonsense.

Michael felt a dozen simultaneous emotions. They arrived all at once; he wasn't ready for them. He threw the sumbook across the room. It slammed against his door and dropped to the floor, facedown. He threw his pillow. He threw a pen. When there was nothing left to throw, he stood up and paced.

Why carry a book that was written in gobbledygook? A book that no one could read?

He hit play on his portable stereo. When the Red Hot Chili Peppers came to life, he turned the volume up full blast and kept walking in circles. His mind turned and turned.

It couldn't be gibberish. That wouldn't make sense, would it?

It had to be written in some kind of code. A code Ridge understood.

Yes, that was it.

It was code. A fail-safe. Just in case someone got their hands on it.

Someone like you, Michael. It's a fail-safe against someone like you.

Michael pushed the thought away. He didn't do anything wrong by stealing the sumbook, did he? He just wanted to be prepared, that's all. He wanted to know what was coming. There were so many potential disasters on the horizon. How else would he protect himself and his mama? That was why he'd stolen the book. That was why he had stolen the canned goods and tools. To put his mind at ease.

Only his mind was never really at ease.

See, *that's* why he needed the book. Once he had read it from cover to cover, he wouldn't be anxious anymore. He'd be ready for whatever life had to throw at him.

He snatched the sumbook off the floor. The pen too. He spied the gum wrapper with "Paige Kaminski" written on it on the carpet, but it drifted out of his mind as soon as he sat down on his bed and got to work.

37

Michael's stomach growled and rumbled, but he didn't notice. His foot had fallen asleep, but it barely registered. The Chili Peppers sang—"Around the World," "Parallel Universe," "Scar Tissue," "Otherside"—over and over and over. How many times? Michael had no idea. He didn't lift his head from the sumbook until he heard three loud knocks on his locked bedroom door. He flinched and noticed a sharp pain at the base of his neck.

His mother's voice was muffled by the door and music. "Michael? What are you doing in there? Why is this door locked?"

He jumped up, turned off the music, and threw open the door.

His mother was in her restaurant clothes. Her purse was still on her shoulder. She peeked inside and gave him a once-over.

"What are you doing?" she asked.

"You're home from work already?" Michael said. His voice was dry and hoarse. He hadn't spoken all day. Hadn't had a drop to drink, either. Or anything to eat.

"It's nine o'clock."

Nine o'clock?

How had that happened?

Michael glanced at his bed. "I was reading."

The sumbook was opened, spine cracked, pencil marks in the margins, surrounded by a scattering of paper. He hadn't cracked the code. Not a single sentence. Not a single word. He'd tried everything. He wasn't even close.

But he could figure it out, couldn't he?

Eventually.

With time.

"You shouldn't play your music so loud," his mother said. "Think of the neighbors."

"You're right," Michael said. "Sorry. I wasn't thinking."

"Are you okay? You seem jumpy."

The truth was, he wanted his mom out of his room so he could get back to the code.

"I'm fine. I'm just tired," he said. "I think I'm gonna go to bed." He faked a yawn, but his mom seemed unconvinced.

"Did you check on Mr. Mosley's nephew, make sure everything's going okay?"

"Oh," Michael said. "Yeah. He's fine."

"It's a shame there was no memorial service, but it's nice, in a way. Now we all have our own last images of him."

Michael glanced at his bed again.

"Are you sure you're okay?" she said.

"Me? Yeah." He cleared his throat. "How was work?"

She paused.

"I took every breath," she said.

I took every breath.

His mom had been saying that for as long as he could remember, but he never paid much attention to it before. Now, as he sat among his scribbled papers in the stillness of his room, the words filled the air. He thought of how the day had passed without him. He'd taken every breath and been unaware of each one. He thought of his empty stomach, the pain in his neck, the cramp in his hand from holding the pencil, which he still clutched. He thought of the sound of his mother banging on his door, which made him think of Beejee, which made him think of Ridge, which made him think of how Ridge had taken the blame for the tools.

Mr. Mosley had kept a jar by his bed, because he thought Michael was a good kid.

Michael wondered . . . *Am I?*

Maybe he was. Maybe he wasn't. Maybe he was many things.

Michael looked up at the water stain.

One thing was certain.

"I am a thief," he said.

He imagined Mr. Mosley at the foot of his bed, repeating something he'd said the last time Michael had seen him. The day he unloaded the dishwasher.

Before you go to sleep at night, ask yourself: was I the best person I could be today?

And now, ugly thoughts: Michael, stealing the sumbook and lying about it. Michael, standing silent with a pocket full of peaches while Jamar was accused of shoplifting. Michael, swiping tools and gummy bears. Michael, choosing canned goods as a memento.

If the answer is no, do better tomorrow.

Michael closed the book. He gathered the papers in both hands, crumpled them up, and carried them to the kitchen to throw away. He walked quietly, so he wouldn't wake his mother. He grabbed the phone on the way back to his room.

Maybe it was too late to call someone.

Maybe it wasn't.

Maybe there was only one way to find out.

38

The next morning, Michael put on his Jordans and thought of all the things he knew about Paige Kaminski. There was a lot you could share with someone over a two-hour conversation.

Her favorite actor was Leonardo DiCaprio. Her favorite movie was *Titanic*. Her favorite band was NSYNC—disappointing, of course, but not unforgiveable. And her favorite food? Pizza, especially with her favorite topping, which was pepperoni. Her favorite animals were otters. He even knew her favorite color, which was teal.

And she knew things about him too, like that he didn't have a favorite actor, his favorite movie was *Raising Arizona*, and his favorite band was, of course, the Red Hot Chili Peppers. His favorite food was his mama's homemade French toast. Favorite animal? Tigers. (Stray cats were his *actual* favorite animal, but tigers sounded cooler.) He wasn't sure what his favorite color was, but he currently liked black, since it was the color of his shoes.

He thought of all this as he floated to Mr. Mosley's apartment, carrying a big paper bag. Birds sang in the courtyard.

The flowerpot was still there. He got the key from its hiding place and unlocked the door.

He wished he could tell Mr. Mosley about Paige Kaminski.

He wished he could ask him about the first time he had called a girl.

He wished he could ask Mr. Mosley to tell him stories— about his first girlfriend, and his first kiss, and did he have any advice?

Michael took a deep breath and set his bag on top of the donation box. His stash hadn't felt that heavy when he first left the house, but after lugging it from one building to another, his arms ached.

It felt good to set everything down.

Michael stepped toward the kitchen counter and picked up the wallet, the one with the Philadelphia Eagles logo emblazoned on the front. He had never had a wallet before.

"I'm going to do better today, Mr. Mosley," he whispered.

39

You can find water anywhere in Fox Run Apartments in Red Knot, Delaware.

There's a swimming pool.

There are working faucets in every unit.

And, after a rainfall, there are puddles. Many puddles.

Michael stood in front of one of them, on the same sidewalk where he'd first met Ridge, holding the sumbook.

You have the future in your hands, Michael. What are you going to do?

He squatted down and placed the book in the water.

It was easier than he'd thought it would be, to let it go.

The book dissolved in less than five seconds. It was incredible, really. It simply disappeared.

As if it had never been.

40

The Prince family lived in apartment 5A. Michael took his time walking there.

He paused when he got to their door. He shook his hands to get rid of his nerves.

I am living in the first state.

He knocked.

He immediately heard a flurry of activity on the other side. Someone—it sounded like Elijah—yelled, "I'll get it!" followed by the *thump-thump-thump* of feet coming to the door, and someone else, maybe Jamar, yelling, "See who it is first!" But the door was already open.

"Hey, Eli," Michael said.

"Hey, Mike—er, Michael. What's up?"

The Prince apartment felt alive. Cartoons on the TV, with Darius watching intently; baseball bats, books, footballs, blankets scattered here and there; music playing quietly from a stereo. Jamar was on the leather sectional, reading. *The Girl Who Loved Tom Gordon*, by Stephen King. He looked up and half waved.

Michael half waved back and motioned toward the basketball on the floor, behind the couch.

"I was just wondering . . . um. Do you wanna play some one-on-one?"

Eli clapped and immediately scooped up the ball. "Yeah! It's boring here. This one's watching stupid cartoons and this one's reading some dumb book about a girl."

"It's not dumb," Jamar said.

"I don't play that much," Michael said. "Or at all, really."

"Good," Eli said, wiggling his foot into one of his sneakers, the ball clamped under his arm. "That means I'll win all the time."

Jamar set his book down and shook his head. "Not very sportsmanlike, Eli."

"Well, you never know," Eli said. He was working on the other sneaker now. He glanced up at Michael. "Maybe you'll be better than you think. What if you're the next Michael Jordan?"

"Yeah," said Michael. "What if?"

Additional excerpts from
THE SPATIAL TELEPORTATION SUMMARY BOOK
(1980–2020)

Written by Maria Sabio, PhD, DST, Chief STS,
University of Delaware
Translated from Original Eaker Linton Code

Elizabeth Gibson-Gray, PhD, the founder of spatial teleportation theory, was born on February 5, 1983. Dr. Gibson-Gray earned a bachelor's degree in engineering, and a master's and doctorate in physics, all from the University of Delaware. Dr. Gibson-Gray developed the initial theories of spatial teleportation—then colloquially known as "time travel"—during her tenure as a quantum physicist at the Massachusetts Institute of Technology. Although her findings were not discovered until after her death, it is well documented that her interest in spatial teleportation began when she was in her teens, after she won a LEGO robotics set in a giveaway and discovered an aptitude for engineering. The LEGO Group used Dr. Gibson-Gray's likeness as part of its advertising for much of the 2180s. The EGG (See *EGG*), the device that makes spatial teleportation possible, is named in her honor.

Streaming television services were introduced in the early 1990s to describe video-on-demand services, but streaming did not fully take off until the mid-2000s, with the continued rise of the internet.

Netflix, a media streaming and video rental service, was introduced in 1997, but did not immediately assimilate into the mainstream. The company launched an initial public offering (IPO) in 2002, which allowed the public to invest, but it was still a fairly modest company at the time. Netflix quickly grew into a behemoth, however. It is estimated that a person who invested $5,000 in Netflix at its 2002 IPO would have about $30,000 by January 2010, about $200,000 by January 2015, and about $1.4 million by January 2020.

One hundred million metric tons of plastic were being produced in the mid-1980s. By 2020, that number increased to 375 million metric tons. During this period, plastic increasingly filled landfills and oceans while its production—up to 8 million tons annually by 2020—contributed to air pollution and greenhouse gas emissions. By the time plastic production ended in 2072, plastic far outweighed all the fish in the sea and was responsible for the extinction and/or endangerment of more than 129 species, including the beluga whale, the Florida manatee, the hawksbill turtle, and sea lions.

✷

The Mosley Conservation Institute (MCI) was founded in 2018 by Delaware natives Michael Rosario and Paige Kaminski-Rosario for the preservation and protection of wilderness and wildlife and the reduction of human impact on the environment. Today, the MCI is the longest-running non-governmental organization dedicated solely to conservation. It has been in continuous operation for more than 150 years. The MCI logo—an entwined tiger and otter—is one of the most recognizable icons in the world.

✷

Summary books are provided by the University of Delaware Spatial Teleportation Sciences Department and designed to protect and educate teleportation scientists as they rematerialize in timeprints that may not support modern technology.